To Yvoni

C000083531

Meet
Peter the Pickpocket

Best Wishes

John Trainor

This book is dedicated to Patrick Harvey, wherever he may be.

OTHER TITLES BY JOHN TRAINOR

AUTHOR'S NOTE

"THERE BUT for the grace of God go I."—John Bradford (circa 1510-1555)

This very profound and touching statement seldom reaches our hearts as we see those less fortunate suffering daily. We often observe situations that are absolutely atrocious, yet most of us choose to turn away.

In the moment, these circumstances may cause us to shudder, but then we rid ourselves of those negative visions, adopting the attitude that "It's well beyond my control. There's nothing I can do about it."

But we must ask ourselves, how much thought do we give to the single mother who struggles to raise her Down syndrome baby? Or to the blind person struggling to cross the busy road? Then there's the person who has been wrongfully convicted and rots in his prison cell with no advocate to defend him.

A case of 'out of sight, out of mind'?

*****

This book could be filled with numerous examples, but if we are not directly involved, we just move on. However, before I move on, I'd like to take this opportunity to recognize those special few in life who *do* stop what they are doing to make a difference.

This story is pure fiction, but I sincerely hope you get a sense that there many injustices in this world, and *your* gesture—no matter how small—can and, at the risk of sounding presumptuous, *will* make a difference to that person who cries out silently for your help.

Whatever unfortunate circumstances you may see, please always remember to quote John Bradford.

"There but for the grace of God go I."

~John Trainor

THE WAY A MAN chooses to make a living is often defined by the circumstances of his birth more than by the options presented to him. Perhaps it would be more accurate to state that you are a product of your environment.

Some might say that Peter Cooney was working class, but that would give the illusion that men who were working class were millionaires. Often, those whom the universe appoints as caretakers are ill-equipped to bring a child to its full potential. Peter Cooney was actually not even working class—he was from a stratum below even a street person or persona non grata. He was from the other side of the tracks and always had a hard-scrabble life, full of unexpected events with meager love and care.

He was, in other words, dirt poor. He did not even own the dirt in his grubby, worn shoes, or the dry coating of clay that clung to his thin, frayed socks. The day his mother gave birth to the bright-eyed boy, court papers were immediately served removing the healthy newborn from his birth parents and placing him into the care of the authorities. This action was to ensure that he wouldn't suffer the same fate as his siblings. The horrendous treatment his older brother and sister endured was trumpeted by three national newspapers. At the conclusion of the trial, a unanimous verdict of guilty was brought against what the judge described as, "The cruelest case of parenting I have ever witnessed in my thirty years on the bench."

People say the road to hell is paved with good intentions, and those who volunteered as foster parents perhaps meant well. Caring for young Peter was challenging for those well-meaning couples who volunteered to create a loving environment for the boy, though for a modest amount of financial compensation they soon had second thoughts. He was a complex child and needed special attention, patience, and compassion.

There was a short probationary period to determine if the child and potential foster parents were a good match, after which many couples decided to forgo care of orphaned children. Sometimes, it was not worth the stress. The few intrepid foster parents who did open their home to young Peter soon regretted allowing him into their lives. With the baby's striking good looks, most couples thought the youngster would be a good fit, however, there was an escape clause inserted into the court documents ensuring that the child could be returned before the probationary period expired. Consequently, the boisterous young Peter was blown around like a leaf, shifted and blown from one pile of misfortune to another.

Though the odds seemed never to favor him, there was one young couple who felt up to the task, and after two years of nurturing the hard-to-handle Peter, they made application to the court to formally adopt. The process was moving along very smoothly, and everything seemed to be in place. An official date was fixed for young Peter to have a place he could call home and finally live with two loving individuals he would recognize as his Mum and Dad.

The future looked bright for all concerned until one dark November evening when a drunk driver ran a red light, crashing into the side of the prospective parents' car and killing them instantly. This sad news meant nothing to baby Peter as he was still at an age where his little world only revolved around having three meals a day and plenty of sleep.

However, the tragic event meant Peter Patrick Cooney would remain in a life of instability, further promoting a nomadic and troubled existence.

Peter's undesirable circumstances lasted until his seventh birthday, when he was removed from yet another set of well-intentioned foster parents. The free-thinking, spirited youngster was placed in an orphanage run by a religious organization that to all intents and purposes had never heard the Sermon on the Mount and the teachings of being God loving. The staff treated the children in their care like prisoners rather than delicate young souls. These young people had been dealt an unfavorable hand in the game of life which is often stacked against those with challenging, difficult, and problematic backgrounds.

The cards were not only stacked against the children residing in this home for "unwanted" kids, it was literally a classic case of Three-Card Monty. The cards were wielded deftly and quickly and none of the children could ever find love or their place in life. The dealers moved the cards with slick hands that inflicted cruelty on their wretched young lives.

"The place is a hold-over from the old Victorian-era labor camps," the local people often said. The orphans were made to stand by their ready-made beds at 6 a.m. preparing for the strenuous day ahead. After the completion of the morning bed inspection, a less-than-substantial breakfast awaited them. Later, the scrubbing and cleaning of the hallway and corridor floors began as well as whatever chores the sadistic regime deemed necessary on that day. The purpose of this laborious exercise was to give the appearance of cleanliness in the unlikely event that unexpected visitors from the Social Work Department came to audit the government-funded home. The men of the cloth responsible for the care of the children had to justify the generous compensation they received for housing society's unwanted. The fact that the floors were squeaky clean reflected well on the establishment and gave the overall impression it was being operated properly. The inspectors never realized that the thugs clothed in the frocks of godly men hoped the institution was being evaluated for its superficial appearances. They hoped they could deceive the auditors with a little polish. The children who were on the receiving end of the sadistic treatment that the church's disciplinarians meted out couldn't envision a bright future for themselves. These children were prisoners in a totalitarian regime that failed to encourage or promote any useful life skills. Their plan was to impart no love or kindness and inflict maximum damage under the guise of a good godly education.

The head honcho of the orphanage was Brother Desmond, a twisted individual with a ruddy face and slack jaw who delighted in seeing kids squirm and suffer. His hair was parted awkwardly down the middle, as if his mum had been in a hurry and had left it slightly crooked and off, just like he was. The more senior residents believed that Brother Desmond was condemned to the orphanage by Lucifer himself. They were of the opinion that he had a return ticket to rejoin his master in the pit of Hell but had created his own Luciferian environment for his charges while awaiting his return to the underworld.

One glance at this man the children had nicknamed "The Commandant" and it was apparent to anyone that Hitler's Gestapo would find his actions unacceptable. Despite his smooth velvet words that could sweeten the most sour and horrid circumstances, he was a sinister manipulator. This veneer was especially prevalent when it came time to tick all the boxes, ensuring the establishment was run in accordance with the law.

On one occasion, young Danny Wilson—who had been in the home since his sixth birthday and had just celebrated his fifteenth—tried to make it known to an inspector that everything within the institutional green walls of this hell wasn't as it seemed. Danny approached one of the gentlemen in a pin-striped suit who looked like he would listen. It was the boy's intention to voice his grievances and as he politely approached, he asked the kind-faced man, "Can I speak to you concerning an important matter?"

The boy was interrupted by Brother Hardy, the Commandant's lieutenant, and ushered away before he could utter another word to the man from the Social Work Department. He was taken to a room where he would pay dearly for his insubordinate behavior. As he was led away, the inspector was unaware of the maneuver that had transpired and smiled. "Perhaps another time, young man."

No sooner had the unsuspecting, well-clad gentleman exited the building than Brother Desmond summoned two of his heavyset thugs to stretch young Danny Wilson across a wooden bench and give him ten good strokes on his buttocks with a three-inch-thick leather strap. Danny's cries and moans echoed through the Victorian corridors of the orphanage until they reached the tender ears of Peter Cooney.

The following morning, the inquisitive seven-year-old Peter asked the oldest boy in the dorm why he was crying. Putting on a brave face, Danny answered, "Oh, it was just a little punishment. I deserved it for misbehaving in front of Brother Desmond."

Peter didn't believe Danny's response and pushed to get an answer that he would find more palatable. The most senior boy in the institution was aware that if he told the truth to the youngster, it might lead to him getting punished again, and also

5

ran the risk of Peter being introduced to his first taste of the dreaded leather strap.

Danny said, "Listen, wee man, and listen good. I'm going to tell you all about this place but not right now. You and I will become good pals, but you mustn't share what I say with any of the rest of them."

This time the big boy's response temporarily satisfied the new kid in town—he could hardly wait to hear all about the inner working of this place they called home. What really excited the youngster was the fact that he had a big brother figure he could look to for guidance.

For the next few weeks Peter and his "Big Brother Danny" became close. Peter even began to mimic Danny's every move. This behavior didn't go unnoticed by the other members of the dormitory and caused the boys more senior than young Cooney to become jealous of the relationship.

On one occasion when they had time for leisure pursuits, Danny saw a ten-year-old wannabe leader getting on about his young pal and giving him a right good hiding. The older boy was throwing punches into the face of young Cooney while another was kicking his adopted brother in the ribs.

Danny ran to rescue his little pal only to be stopped by Brother Desmond—obviously the sadistic man had orchestrated the entire mismatch. "Danny, don't go any further. If you do, you can rest assured that the beating your little friend is getting will be a picnic in comparison to what you will be receiving."

Feeling helpless, Danny decided to literally take matters into his own hands. He turned to confront the man he despised most in this world and hit him with a right hook to the jaw that sent him sprawling across the gymnasium floor. Before the devil could get up, Danny gave him a swift kick in the ribs, far greater than the ones being meted out to his young pal. The blow to his midsection ensured that Brother Desmond would not be giving out retributions to innocent children again anytime soon.

Confident the head of the house wasn't going anywhere, Danny jumped into the circle and pulled the two bullies off his young friend. Having rescued Peter from the ruffians, he turned to see if Brother Desmond had regained consciousness. He was surprised that not only had he come to his senses but was moving towards him with what looked like a lynch mob. He grabbed young Peter's hand and the two raced across the gymnasium towards an open door which led to the main entrance. Their timing could not have been better since the gate had been left ajar by the local grocer making a delivery.

2

DOORS LEFT AJAR can be a misrepresentation for a door of opportunity. What at first may be seen as a means of escape, can often lead to situations more dire than the place that has been exited. It is not until we embark on a journey that we become like errant fools or cats being scattered by the barking of wild dogs.

Danny and Peter scampered down Graham Street and only time would tell if their decision to bolt was wise or foolhardy. They were pursued by their tormentors but because they were street-smart, they soon blended into the crowd of city dwellers trudging to their dull and meaningless jobs and loveless lives. The older fugitive knew it wouldn't be long before there would be a police presence thicker than the cold, dirty fog that enveloped the city each morning. They would be on every street corner, some in plain clothes and others parading around in badly pressed police uniforms. But how could Danny convey his anxiety and dread of the labyrinth of resistance their escape would encounter? How would a look let young Peter realize the enormity of their predicament and the severity of their punishment should they be apprehended?

Danny was a razor-sharp kid and had often dreamt of the moment when he'd be in the thick of the adventure. He had evaded the authorities and was living by his wits. Having survived the rough life of the orphanage, the escape seemed to be a victory because he was now free from the control of the wolves in sheep's clothing. This wasn't his first foray into freedom. In fact, it was his fourth escape from the hell in which he lived. But he was optimistic that this time he would not be returning to the prison orphanage and its imposing and menacing walls.

On the other hand, Peter gave no thought to the dire consequences of his actions and what it might mean for his future life. He was enjoying every minute of the adventure. As they made their way towards Glasgow central train station, Peter asked innocently, "Danny, can we go to France? I've never been."

The leader of the escapees was more mature than his age would suggest and replied, "Peter, my wee pal, for the time being, let's forget about France. Let's just get as far from this hell-hole as possible."

No sooner had Danny responded to Peter's inquiry than he observed two portly officers coming towards them. Quickly grabbing the youngster's hand, Danny urged his friend across the busy street, dodging oncoming traffic. They made their way down the steps to the station platforms. It was more than obvious that the two uniformed officers would not be trying out for the Olympics anytime soon. The rotund pursuers recognized the youngsters as the orphanage fugitives and gave chase, however they were no match for the adrenalin racing through the legs of the runaways. Mingling with the busy commuters, the boys skittered ahead and boarded an inter-city express. They were now out of sight of the panting and gasping lawmen. The officers realized they were pursuing quick and elusive phantoms and used their radios for assistance, but even this proved pointless in their plight to apprehend the fleeing youths.

The boys were filled with a sense of relief and at last felt secure in the fact that the non-stop express was pulling away from the platform and gathering momentum. Delighted to be onboard, they hoped eventually to be transported to eternal freedom. Having no clue where the express was heading, Danny overheard two old ladies talking.

"Do you travel to London often?" said one to the other.

"No," replied the older woman, "not since Johnny, my husband of fifty-four years, passed away."

Danny now knew where he and his ticketless friend were destined. Being the leader of the excursion, he told Peter to follow him through the train—he had a plan to dodge the ticket inspector. Reaching the end of one of the carriages, he saw the 'vacant' sign on the door of the toilet. The two jumped in quickly and slid the latch to the locked position. Danny sat on the toilet seat like the chairman at a board meeting and disclosed his master plan, giving his young accomplice instructions in a low voice.

"Okay, pal, this is what we'll do. When the ticket inspector knocks on the door asking for tickets, you say 'Mr., I'm doing a number two. My Mum and Dad have my ticket.'"

Peter questioned the plan-maker's authority. "Danny, why don't *you* say that your Mum and Dad have your ticket?"

Danny showed remarkable patience and maturity as he whispered, "Because my voice sounds too grown-up. When he hears *your* voice, he'll be more convinced."

Just as Danny delivered the plan, right on cue three knocks sounded on the door. The authoritative voice of the ticket collector asked for their proof of fare. "Tickets, please!"

Danny nudged his young accomplice. Remembering his lines, Peter responded exactly as they had rehearsed.

To Danny's delight, the inspector replied, "That's okay, son, don't forget to wash your hands when you're done."

Danny nudged Peter and gestured with his hand, telling the boy to thank the man. Peter picked up on his big brother's prompting and said, "Okay, sir, thank you."

The two boys remained still then to be sure the coast was clear. After a while, Danny lay on the toilet floor to peer through the tiny gap under the door to ensure there weren't two big, black railway issue boots obstructing the light.

Confident that all was well, they opened the door and casually walked toward the restaurant car. Seeing a vacant table, Danny said to Peter, "Stay here. I'll do the talking."

Before he could leave the table, the restaurant car waiter greeted the boys. "Well, gentlemen, would you like to see the wine list?" The waiter's cocky and sarcastic tone led Danny to reply, "No, thank you. Our Mum and Dad wouldn't approve. But can we have two sodas until they join us?"

The accommodating old waiter replied, "Would you like something to eat before they come or are you going to wait and eat together?"

Peter kicked his partner's leg under the table and said, "Johnny, let's just start without them. Dad did say we can have whatever we want since it's my birthday."

The waiter smiled and asked, "And what age is our young passenger today then?"

Danny, impressed with his young brother's move, replied, "He's five."

The waiter ruffled Peter's hair and said, "You're very big for five, young man."

Taking the lead, Danny said, "Everyone says that he takes after my Dad—he's six-feet-four."

Removing his notebook from his pocket and licking the point of a very worn-down pencil, the waiter said, "Well, we have two sodas…and what would you like to eat?"

In unison they answered, "Hamburgers and chips, please."

"Two hamburgers and chips coming right up." Impressed with the boys' manners, the waiter added, "You boys are so well-mannered—your parents should be very proud of you."

In unison they said, "Thank you, sir."

After the waiter had gone, the boys burst into a fit of giggles. Their laughter lasted till the waiter came with their order.

"There you go, two sodas and two hamburgers and chips. Boys, I also have a little birthday cake, but let's save that till your parents join you."

As the likable waiter walked away, Danny blurted, "It may be a while before Mum and Dad get here!"

That started another bout of laughter. The boys wasted no time tucking into their free meal. Between mouthfuls of burgers and fries they chatted about how life was going to be away from the orphanage.

Just then, Danny glanced down the center aisle of the restaurant car and almost choked. To his horror, he saw the ticket inspector. The man wearing the official railway cap was holding what looked to be a ticket punch and was making his way towards them. They heard him making inquiries to the other passengers.

"Excuse me, Sir and Madam, by any chance did you happen to see a young boy aged about five or six?"

An elderly couple who had slept most of the journey awoke and the gentleman was none too happy to be disturbed. "No, we've not noticed anybody. We just want to rest, if you don't mind. We would thank you kindly to not bother us."

Happy to avoid any further reprimand from the sleeping pensioners, he saw his friend the waiter walking towards him.

"Charlie, did you happen to see a kid traveling alone? He's about five or six."

"No, Dave, I haven't seen any child that fits that description." He hesitated and said, "Oh, wait a minute. There are two young boys sitting in the middle of the restaurant car tucking into big, juicy hamburgers. One was five—it's his birthday. He's with his parents and an older brother."

The waiter's reply halted the ticket inspector's search. Being privy to the conversation, the young fugitives crouched down behind the high-backed seat wondering if the game was up. Danny peeked out and saw the man who continued his search for a five-year-old. The boys were relieved to see him turn around and make his way back to the carriage car.

Peter sensed that Danny was no longer in a mood to giggle. "Danny, Danny, where to now? What are we going to do?"

Danny felt he had to devise a new master plan and quickly came up with a strategy that would put his young companion's mind to rest. "I'm not too sure, Peter, but I know one thing. We ain't staying here. Let's get out of these seats and make our way through the carriages toward the front of the train."

Peter asked incredulously, "Then what?"

Danny responded, "Then what? I don't have a clue." His tone was steeped in irritation.

They were cautiously making their way towards the front of the train when it suddenly and unexpectedly jerked to a halt. This caused the immaculately starched table covers and settings to crash to the floor in a riotous clang and crack of dishes and glasses. This was the perfect distraction for the boys to exit.

After they vacated the car, Peter began to wonder if the excursion was over. Then the Glasgow-to-London Express began to pull away. That is when the two non-paying passengers knew the game would not soon be coming to a sudden and tragic end. Now it was a race against time. The ticket inspector's shadow would soon be looming right next to them.

When they found themselves in the first-class section of the train, they occupied two vacant seats. Danny made every effort to blend in with the other well-heeled travelers. "Excuse me, sir," he inquired, "when will we be arriving in London?"

Young Peter's diminutive tour guide posed this question to an unsuspecting commuter. The well-dressed business gent with a waxed mustache checked his gold Albert pocket watch and replied, "Anytime now, young man. However, if it wasn't for the stray cattle on the line we would be there already."

The gentleman's answer was music to Danny's ears. Peter tugged at his surrogate brother's shirt and asked, "Danny, what did he say? Will we be there soon?"

Before Danny could answer the question, the train's momentum began to diminish. As they looked out the window, they could see they were approaching London's Kings Cross Station.

They would have nowhere to hide and the ticket inspector would catch them! Danny knew if they tried to hide in the bathroom they would be caught and have no escape.

"Hey, you two, come here!" the aging inspector shouted from the far end of the last carriage. Fortunately for the two young fugitives, right at that moment the train hit the buffers. The disembarking passengers were preoccupied gathering their luggage and belongings and were not aware of why the ticket inspector was shouting. Just as they were ready to dart from the locomotive, an authoritative voice of a soldier in uniform said, "Not so fast, boys. Where are your manners? Can't you see the lady in front of you?"

Danny politely apologized to the man who displayed three stripes on his neatly pressed uniform. Meanwhile, the ticket inspector was desperately trying to weave his way through the crowded passageway in hopes of capturing the free-riding youngsters.

3

EVEN THE BEST of clairvoyants cannot be sure that their projections will be accurate. For Danny and young Peter, to foresee what lay ahead of them was unimaginable.

Danny suspected that by now every bobby in the greater Metropolitan London area was on the lookout for them from north of the border. He decided on the youngster's behalf that they should go where they would not look out of place.

"Danny, I need a pee and I'm starving," complained Peter.

Danny knew it would be too risky to hang around the station, so he urged Peter to hold his pee for five minutes. "Peter, do me a favor, pal. Hold it for just a wee while more, till we get out of the station. Then I'll find you a place to pee."

Reluctantly, Peter of the full bladder agreed to his mentor's request. As soon as they left the station, Danny was true to his word. "Okay, Pal, there's a bathroom over there. I'm bursting, too, so let's have a right good piss."

Peter looked up to the almost-six-foot youth and asked, "Then can we get something to eat?"

"One thing at a time. Let's get a pee first, then we'll see about something to eat."

Danny's caring tone gave Peter a level of comfort he'd yet to experience in his short but traumatic life.

After both bladders had been drained, the next challenge was to fill their empty bellies. They stood at a park in the middle of nowhere and could see a bright illuminated sign of a fast food restaurant in the distance. Danny scratched his greasy hair and adjusted his proverbial survival cap. "Come on, pal, let's go. I have an idea."

His obedient sidekick followed his hero to the packed fast food restaurant. When they entered, the smell caused their mouths to water. Finding a seat, Danny took note of what was going on. When the orders were ready, someone from behind the busy counter would shout out the number and leave the tray full of delicious fries and burgers for a pre-paid customer to pick up.

As the procedure continued, the boys' hunger pangs grew by the second. Taking it all in, Danny devised a plan. "Okay, Peter, here's what we'll do. When the girl calls out a number and we see it has enough food on the tray, if no one seems in a hurry to collect it, you go to the counter and pick it up. If you're asked for a receipt, say your big brother is in the bathroom with the ticket. If she doesn't say anything just bring the tray over to this seat by the door. I'll be waiting for you. Then we'll walk out with our dinner."

Peter barely had time to consider his accomplice's plan when the number "603" was called. It was in an accent unfamiliar to his young Glaswegian ears and the girl who called the number certainly did not look like she was from Glasgow. It was obvious she must have been from one of the Caribbean islands with her thick, flowing tangled dreads and colorful green, black and yellow garb. She repeated her sing-song call, reminiscent of Harry Belafonte's *The Banana Boat*.

Danny urged Peter, "Okay, pal, go and get it! Remember, if she asks for the ticket, your big brother is in the bathroom."

The plan worked like clockwork—almost. Peter stepped up to the counter prepared to take the tray and found himself next to an elderly gentleman who was also collecting his order. Seeing the old man's wallet protruding from his back pocket—and finding the temptation impossible to resist—Peter put out his hand to snatch it.

Belying his age and stooped shoulders, the observant old man quickly grabbed Peter's wrist. With his eyes boring into the young man's face, he growled, "What's your name, son?"

Raising his gaze to the man's scowl, Peter envisioned the police dragging him away and locking him behind bars. In a quick movement, he yanked his hand free of the man's grasp, snatched the tray, and dashed to the table where Danny was waiting.

Although unaware of his young accomplice's close call, he wasted no time putting the contents of the tray into a plastic bag he'd found on the floor near the condiments. In military-like fashion, he gave the order. "Let's go! You carry the drinks; I've got everything else."

Peter was in an even bigger hurry than his friend to vacate the premises and nearly spilled the drinks on his way out the door.

"What's your rush, Peter? We're home free—the plan worked."

Ashamed, Peter confessed that he'd nearly been caught with his hand in the cookie jar.

"Okay, pal," Danny said, "no spur-of-the-moment chances—even if it looks easy. Got it?"

"Yes, I get it." Then he whined, "Danny, I'm starving. Can we eat now?"

"Just another minute, pal. I think the rain is ready to pour down. Let's cross the road to that bus shelter and we'll stay dry."

Sitting on the wooden bench in the comfort of the London transport bus shelter, Peter said, "Danny, I thought the burger on the train was good, but this is far better, and the chips are definitely crispy."

Danny didn't acknowledge Peter's opinion regarding the quality of the cuisine—he was preoccupied juggling his soda and a handful of free dinner. The rain came down in torrents and they were both happy to be sheltered from the torrential London deluge.

The seven-year-old Peter was forever living in the moment, so he had never stopped to think where he would be laying his wee Scottish head for the night. Then the thought suddenly occurred to him. "Danny, do you know anybody in London we could go live with?"

In his strong brogue, he replied, "Aye, the fuckin' Queen!"

Peter, in his innocence, believed for a second that his big hero was serious. He then saw him start to laugh and they went into their habitual giggling routine. Before the laughing stopped, they noticed a man leaving a nearby telephone box and running toward the bus shelter to get out of the rain. After shaking the excess water from his cream-colored raincoat, he heard the boys speak and immediately knew they were from Glasgow.

The stranger's accent equaled theirs. "Where in the toon are ye boys from?"

Danny, conscious that the man could be an undercover police officer, replied in a cheeky tone, "Who's asking?"

The Glaswegian appreciated the boy's fortitude and sarcastically replied, "Inspector Jimmy Clouseau, the famous Scottish detective. Naw, wait a wee minute, he wis a Frenchman."

Hearing the man putting on a French accent over his heavy, west-of-Scotland brogue caused the runaways to burst into a fit of hilarity.

Then Jimmy continued. "Listen to me, boys. It's written all over yer faces. You boys are on the run."

Danny defensively retorted, "Wit makes ye say that?"

Exhaling his cigarette smoke, he replied, "A wasn't born yesterday, son, and besides, a did wit yer doin' years ago."

Danny took one look at what appeared a very streetwise Glaswegian and decided he should seek the help of his fellow countryman. Having walked the same path that the boys were now experiencing, the man who was taking cover from the rain appreciated the plight of the two young fugitives.

"Okay, you're right. We are on the run and have nowhere to go. Can you help us?" Danny was confessing in the hope that the Good Samaritan would take pity on them and come to their aid. As he was pleading their case, Peter was busy slurping on his straw and trying to get the last of his soda from the bottom of the cup.

After sizing up the boys' situation, Jimmy decided he would rescue them from their predicament. Before initiating his philanthropic deed, he began a line of questioning. "Before I help you, tell me all about yourselves and what you have been up to." Jimmy began his interrogation and Danny started to second guess whether he should spill the beans or dish them out in small installments. Taking a deep breath, he adopted an all-or-nothing attitude.

"Okay, Jimmy, I'll tell you everything, but if you grass on us I'll never forget that you did. When I grow up, I'll come looking for ye."

Jimmy reacted as if it was a grown man giving the threat. "Listen, arse-hole. Don't threaten me with what you'll do or not do." Jimmy opened his overcoat and pulled out what seemed to be a Second World War revolver. "Arse-hole, see that? I'll blow yer fuckin' head off if you give me anymore of yer cheek."

Peter had been preoccupied with the last of his soda, but he almost swallowed the straw when he saw Jimmy's gun and heard him threaten Danny. The man with the 1942 German Luger saw the fear in the young boy's eyes and softened his tone. "It's okay, ma wee man, everything is cool as long as yer big brother learns a wee bit of respect and knows when to shut his mouth."

Danny quickly apologized and said, "I'm sorry, mister, I didn't mean to be cheeky. It's just that we ran away from an orphanage in Glasgow and we've no money and nowhere to go."

Peter was surprised to see tears trickling down his hero's cheeks. He stepped close and pressed into Danny's waist. "It's okay, Danny. Please, don't hurt us, Mister. We don't want to go back to that place."

Seeing that both boys were in a world of hurt, Jimmy said, "Okay, okay. Let's just cool it for a minute. I'll take you back to my place—you can stay there for a few nights till we get you sorted out."

Danny interrupted Jimmy in a very quiet and apologetic voice. "Jimmy, I'm not being cheeky. But what do you mean, 'get us sorted out'?"

Jimmy smiled and said sarcastically, "It's okay, big man. I'm not goin' to grass on you. I don't want you coming after me when you grow up. Naw, what we're goin' to do is get you organized. Ye never need to go back to that place."

Jimmy put the boys' minds at rest. Just then a double-decker bus arrived that would take them to his house near Soho Square. The ticket collector was black, and Peter noticed she had the same accent as the lady from whom he had stolen their dinner.

"Where to, darlin'?" she asked.

"One adult and two kids to Soho Square, please." The large, black ticket collector looked at Danny and then at Jimmy and said, "You sure he's a kid? He's the biggest kid I've ever seen."

Danny, humorous as ever, said, "All my family is big, just look at my feet. My Dad was nearly seven feet tall."

Jimmy confirmed Danny's statement and added, "The sad thing is that his Dad is no longer with us. He died in a horrible road accident up in Scotland last week."

The nosy lady from the Caribbean began looking for particulars regarding the accident, but Jimmy cut her short. "With all due respect, lady, the boy doesn't really want to talk about it right now."

"Oh, of course. Pardon me," she said, ruffling her large dark hands through Danny's hair.

As she made her way back down the stairs, Jimmy turned to the boys. "You boys are going to learn an awful lot over the next couple of days."

"Soho Square" echoed through the bus from the lower deck. As the three Glaswegians made their way downstairs, the big-hearted ticket collector pressed two shillings into Danny's hand. "I'm really sorry about what happened to your Daddy, love. But you get yourself and your little brother some sweets."

4

IN CONTEMPLATING the unexpected, we often develop a pessimistic attitude, because we envision the dreadful and therefore create darkness instead of light.

The boys followed Jimmy to the place he referred to as his London residence and they could not believe the man they had met at the bus shelter resided in such affluence. As they approached the entrance, a uniformed doorman decked out in his immaculate bottle-green hat and tails tipped his hat. "Good evening, Gov, I see you have young guests tonight."

"Yes, Charlie, these are my nephews from Glasgow. They'll be with me for a week or two. You know, for the old school holidays."

Jimmy's comments excited them. Two full weeks in such splendor! An hour earlier Danny had been in a turmoil wondering where they were going to spend their first night in the capital. Now, here they were, about to enter the lap of luxury.

Entering the private elevator, Danny smiled. "Uncle Jimmy, how did you manage to get this place?"

In a semi-reprimanding tone, the man replied, "Young man, ask no questions, and you'll be told no lies."

Danny was a fast learner and knew to take his London uncle's advice to heart.

The private elevator led them directly to Jimmy's luxurious apartment. Both boys were gob smacked. Peter couldn't believe what he was seeing. "Jimmy, I've never seen a place like this before, not even on the television. Can we stay here forever?"

"Who have we here?" The question came from the deep, sultry voice of a leggy blond who sat in a dimly lit room. She held a champagne glass and was dressed in a black lace garment that could be described as filmy at best.

The master of the house said, "Cynthia, these are my newfound Glasgow buddies. They'll be with us for two or three days."

Danny looked at Peter, who had a puzzled expression on his tired face. He was trying to work out what was going on. Jimmy had just told the uniformed doorman they'd be here for a week or two; now he tells the sultry blond they'd be here for two or three days. Danny took Jimmy's advice and thought it best not to question his host. He was grateful in the knowledge that he and his wee pal would have a nice comfortable place to sleep for the night and they wouldn't be rising to make the 6 a.m. roll call.

Before the boys were taken to their palatial suite, Jimmy showed his guests around the penthouse apartment. He then asked what they'd like for supper.

Peter had gotten into the habit of calling his host Uncle Jimmy. "Uncle Jimmy, I've never had supper in my life. I know you can get a fish supper in the chip shop, but I've never heard of supper before going to bed."

Jimmy looked at the boy. "Well, wee man, you're going to have supper tonight. What would you like? Just say the word and I'll make sure you have it."

Peter turned to his mentor and asked, "Danny, what would you like?"

The boys pondered for a minute and finally Danny said, "You know what I'd really, really love? But, I'm not sure if you can get it for us."

Curious to hear what it was, Jimmy said, "Tell me, I bet I can get it."

Half teasing, the boy said, "Are you sure?"

"If you don't hurry up and tell me, the two of you will go to bed hungry. Now, tell me what you'd like."

Jimmy's urging motivated Danny to speak up. "A big pizza with plenty of everything on it."

The man smiled. "A piece of cake."

"No, a pizza," Danny quipped.

"You're quite the comedian—a likable, funny bastard. Don't ask me why, but I like you." He lifted the phone and called the Concierge. "Mr. Ramsay, please call Tony at the Rainbow Pizza House and arrange for one extra-large pizza to be delivered ASAP. Tell them to put the works on it."

Meanwhile, Jimmy's female friend said to Peter in a thick cockney accent, "'ow old a ye, my little Scottish friend?"

He sheepishly replied, "I'm seven, Miss."

"And what's your name?" she asked softly, turning to Peter.

"Peter Cooney, Miss."

Jimmy yelled, "Cynthia, what is this—a fuckin' quiz? Leave him alone. He's had a tiring day."

Just then the elevator door opened, and another uniformed gentleman decked out in the same green tails and top hat said, "I have your pizza order, Sir."

Jimmy slipped some rolled up notes into the man's hand that would more than cover the cost of the pizza and said, "Thanks, George. I hope you didn't eat a slice on the way up."

The gentleman addressed Jimmy as if he was a soldier speaking to a superior officer. "Absolutely not, Sir, but it does smell awfully good."

The boys could smell the pizza from their room and came trotting out to enjoy the largest pie they had ever seen. They ate their fill and there was still half a pizza remaining. It was late, so they said goodnight and went to bed where they would have the best sleep of their young lives.

***

"It's ten o'clock in the morning and the day's half over. Are you two lazy bastards going to lay in bed all day?"

"No, Uncle Jimmy, I'm getting up now."

The older man was starting to enjoy being called Uncle by young Peter.

The ever-attentive host said, "Okay, my boys. What would you like for breakfast?"

They could smell the frying bacon and Danny replied, "Whatever you have would be great."

Focusing his attention on wee Peter, the surrogate uncle said, "And what about you, wee man? What do you fancy?"

Peter imitated everything Danny did and replied, "Can I have the same as Danny, please?"

Jimmy looked at Peter and felt a tremendous sense of obligation to do all he could for the youngster.

During breakfast, Jimmy really got in and about the two boys, asking them a barrage of questions. How did they meet? How did they manage to escape from the orphanage? The most pressing question was, why had they ended up in the orphanage in the first place?

As the question-and-answer session was finishing, Jimmy said, "Danny, you said you'll soon be sixteen. What's your plan for the future?"

Danny had not expected to be quizzed about his future, so he replied, "I don't know. I haven't really thought about it."

"You don't know? Bloody hell, I'd suggest that you better start knowing. Start knowing right now."

Danny listened to Jimmy's harsh reality check and had no clue what to say or do next.

Then Jimmy made a suggestion that gave the boy hope for the future—something to strive towards. In a more fatherly and concerned tone, he said. "When we first met, you confessed you were on the run and had nowhere to go. Here's what I'm going to do for you." Jimmy gazed across the table into Peter's sad eyes as he was about to deliver his master plan to Danny and said, "Don't you worry, wee man, I'll get to you in a minute." Then, returning his attention to Danny, he posed the question. "Okay, if you could be anything, what would you like to be?"

Jimmy had expected Danny to answer the probing inquiry but was taken by surprise when he immediately replied, "A chef." Then, for emphasis, he repeated his answer. "Jimmy, I want to be a chef."

"Well, then, a chef you shall be. I know the head guy in one of the biggest hotels in London and he owes me a huge favor. I'll call him later today." Confidently, Peter's Uncle Jimmy said, "Danny boy, you'll have job by tomorrow morning."

Young Danny was stunned at his turn in fortune. Then the soon-to-be chef said to Jimmy, "I don't have any money or a place to live."

"Yes, you have," his surrogate uncle replied. "I'll get all that arranged today."

Uncle Jimmy was fast becoming the Glaswegian knight in shining armor—a modern-day genie converting their wishes and needs into reality.

He then diverted his attention to the person he always referred to as 'the wee man.' "Now, let's see what we're going to do for you."

Suddenly Peter burst into uncontrollable tears and screamed, "Please, Uncle Jimmy, don't send me back to the orphanage!"

Hearing the boy's heartfelt plea, Jimmy ran to comfort the anxious lad. Holding the child, he said, "Wee man, that's the last place you're going. You're staying here. We'll get you enrolled in a new school and maybe even give you a new name."

Danny had been observing and could not believe what was occurring. He was reluctant to question Jimmy, especially after the incident at the bus stop where he had been told not to ask too many questions. But Danny's curiosity got the better of him and he blurted, "Jimmy, I'm sorry for askin'. But why are you helping us? I've never had anyone help me the way you're doin'."

"Okay," Jimmy said, "I'm going to tell you the reason I have become your guardian angel. It is a coincidence that the same orphanage you escaped from is where I spent many of my own horrible days and nights. I received the same treatment you did from that old bastard they call Brother Desmond. Let me tell you a story about him. Did you happen to notice that he walked with a limp?"

"Yes, of course I did." Danny replied.

"Well, it was I who gave him that limp."

"How, Uncle Jimmy? How did you give him the limp?" asked the curious Peter.

Jimmy refilled his empty mug with fresh tea and continued with the tale of Brother Desmond. "It was a bitter cold day in December—not just ice cold, but bone chilling with a fierce, freezing wind. That bastard told me to go outside. He made me take off my shirt and shovel snow. I begged him to allow me to keep my shirt and jacket on. He told me I had to clear the driveway first without my shirt and jacket."

He took another sip of tea and continued. "My shirt was hanging on a pole right next to where I was shoveling. I shoveled until I couldn't stand it anymore and then put it on. You can imagine, I was fuckin' freezing. Just as I finished putting my clothes on, I saw he was coming at me with a big, heavy stick. He hit me on the arse with it and I fell. The momentum he created when he hit me caused him to slip. I grabbed the stick from him and wanted to smash his stupid head into bits of bone and brains. I thought I might kill him if I hit him in the head, so instead I smacked him on his knees with all the strength I could muster. After that, I did exactly what you two did and ran like hell away from the place."

Danny was fascinated with Jimmy's story. "Did you ever see him again?"

"Oh, yes. I made it a point to see the bastard. I knew he liked a good drink and what bar he frequented. One night about six years ago, myself and, let's say a few friends, paid a visit to that bar. He was standing with a half empty glass and I said to the barman, 'Barman, can you give this man a drink?' The bastard turned around to reply coarsely, 'No, thank you.'

"I told him that I insisted and if he refused I'd stick the glass in his face. He gave me a right good stare and said, 'Do I know you?' I answered, 'I'm not sure. The last time we met it was a very cold December day and you had me take my shirt off to shovel snow.' Then I whispered into his ear, 'Desmond, my friend, you and I are taking a walk. Should you open your mouth, I'll shoot you in the head right where you stand. If you decide to accept my invite, I promise that you will live.'"

"What happened next, Uncle Jimmy?" asked Peter.

"You're a bit young, wee man, to hear what happened next." Jimmy looked at Danny and said, "To hell with it. I'll tell you. Me and my friends took the big cheese of the orphanage outside to very cold and snowy Glasgow Park. I had him completely strip and roll around in the snow. To top it off, I shot him in the back of the same knee where I had cracked him with the stick."

He shook his head and said, "Boys, I'm sorry if my story was a wee bit gruesome." Turning to Peter he said, "Remember, wee man, no one fucks with your Uncle Jimmy."

IT IS SAID, "Too many cooks spoil the broth." However, on many occasions when those in need cry out for a crust, suddenly the kitchen becomes deserted.

Danny was now working in the kitchen of one of London's most prestigious hotels and was enjoying a first-class apprenticeship in the culinary arts.

The next challenge facing Jimmy was what to do with 'the wee man.'

Jimmy was the boys' hero from north of the border. But they did not comprehend the deep implications of the saying, "A wolf in sheep's clothing." They had no clue who the man they held in such high esteem really was.

Although he'd confessed his humble beginnings to the boys, Jimmy Trotter went to great lengths to make sure his dark side went undetected. Even those who thought they knew him had no idea who the real Jimmy Trotter was. He was a man who displayed the perfect example of being all things to all men. One day he would be rubbing shoulders with the city's elite and that night he would be lurking in the darkness with the most notorious of criminals. In most circles, he was known simply as "Jimmy the well-to-do Scotsman." Yet no one seemed to know just how and where their friend had accumulated his substantial wealth. Only one person truly knew the answer to that little secret and that was Jimmy Trotter himself—if that was even his name.

He owned several residences and the likable cavalier never settled in any particular domain for any length of time. His well-stamped passport indicated he had a fondness for sunnier climates, this reflected in the perpetual glow from his bronzed complexion. Anytime Jimmy left his Soho apartment, young Peter was given strict instructions not to answer the phone and remain indoors until his Uncle returned.

Initially, the arrangement suited the young Glaswegian—after all, he was living in one of the finest properties in London. He had access to fifty-six television channels, not to mention a fridge full of all the food he felt like eating. However, after a while the luxurious lifestyle began to grow stale for young master Cooney.

One afternoon as he looked down from the eighth-floor penthouse suite, he began to wonder how it would feel to stroll the busy streets of the city. At that moment, he made the conscience decision to disobey his uncle's strict instructions and decided to take the lift to the ground floor. As he was about to enter the apartment's private elevator and press the button that would deposit him on the busy streets of the city, he was surprised to be met by Jimmy and another one of his many lady friends.

"Wee man, this is Julie."

Doing his utmost to disguise his sheepish face for the actions that he'd been about to take, Peter looked up at the very attractive five-foot-ten blonde and wondered, "Are all my Uncle's friends tall blond ladies?"

"Julie will be your in-house schoolteacher until I can arrange for you to attend a proper school."

Jimmy recognized that young Master Cooney wasn't thrilled about the prospect of being home schooled and asked the boy,

"Peter, if I had ten apples and gave six away, then I bought three more, how many apples would I have?"

Peter struggled to keep up with his uncle's simple mathematical equation and then replied in a dismissive tone, "How would I know?"

Becoming slightly irritated with Peter's dismissive, devil-may-care response, Jimmy raised his voice and said, "Listen, smart-arse, you don't know shit, and that's why I've asked this nice lady to come here and help you become educated."

The youngster was experiencing a side of his Uncle that he preferred not to see and immediately adopted a more compliant attitude. "I'm sorry, Uncle Jimmy. I won't ever act like that again."

Hearing the wee man's confession brought a lump to the benevolent provider's throat. This was a man who had encounters with some of the hardest criminals and had done serious prison time, yet somehow his "wee pal" could reduce the hardened six-foot man to tears.

Ever since he was Peter's age, Jimmy Trotter had had an aptitude for overcoming most challenges life presented. A seven-year-old with the soft misty eyes of a doe needed loving care. This created a situation that Jimmy found not just challenging but verging on the impossible.

Santa Claus was unknown to Peter; in fact, the closest encounter he'd ever had with him was on television. Only ten days remained until Saint Nick was scheduled to ride into the night sky with his illustrious reindeer and deliver presents to every kid in London. Jimmy racked his brain to ensure that this year the wee man would have the best Christmas ever.

He gladly inquired, "What would you like for Christmas, wee man?"

Peter had never been asked this question before and gave Jimmy an answer he least expected.

"Uncle Jimmy, I'd like to be with you for the rest of my life."

Not wanting to disappoint the seven-year-old's request, he made light of it saying, "Santa Claus may not have that in his sack but what he does have is…" But before the philanthrope could elaborate, the boy interrupted him.

"Okay, if Santa Claus can't let me stay with you, could he at least not send me back to the orphanage?"

Jimmy found the conversation difficult to handle and was on the ropes and ready to throw in the towel of surrender. It was at this point that the tall blond teacher came to their rescue.

"I have an idea. Why don't the three of us go to Harrods and talk to Santa about it? We can have dinner and see the Christmas lights in Piccadilly Circus."

Peter was not aware that such places existed, and the images of Harrods' breathtaking Christmas displays were lost on him.

It was the distraction Jimmy needed to hatch a plan for his adopted nephew's future. They were about to leave the apartment when Julie whispered to Jimmy, "Does the boy have any other clothes?"

As caring as Jimmy was he had never given any consideration to the boy's attire. "Oh, my God, Julie, I never thought about that."

Jimmy quickly suggested, "Okay, wee man, before we go anywhere, let's toss those rags you're wearing and buy you some decent clothes. Besides, Santa Claus likes to see all the wee boys and girls looking sharply dressed."

Jimmy brought the boy to one of London's high-class children's outfitters. The young Glasgow orphan could have been the star in the Scottish performance of Pollyanna.

He was now dressed in the finest clothes imaginable and was almost unrecognizable, now ready to meet the white-bearded Saint Nick whose voice echoed from the grotto where he was dispensing gifts and laughter.

"Ho, ho, ho, little chap." The cockney version of Father Christmas greeted Peter amiably. "Now, what would you like for Christmas, my little friend?"

After hearing the Glasgow runaway's response, the overweight part-time Santa almost fell off his red velvet throne.

"Santa, what I'd really like is to live with my Uncle Jimmy for the rest of my life. If I can't have that I would like not to ever go back to the orphanage."

The little girl standing in line behind the boy with the unusual accent and request, turned to her well-heeled parents and asked, "Daddy, what's an orphanage?"

Santa Claus sensed the emotion in the wee man's voice. He had never heard such a request in his twenty-six years of seasonal employment. He felt even more awkward as Peter's eyes began to tear. He ruffled the boy's hair and offered these comforting words: "Everything will be just fine, son."

Breaking the tension, the man in red gave another three cries of his signature, "Ho, ho, ho," and then reached deep into his red ruffled bag and pulled out a large gift. It was wrapped in exquisite paper and contained a surprise that justified the twenty-one pounds that Jimmy had paid to ensure that Peter's first experience with the man from the North Pole was memorable. The contents of the gift box didn't seem to interest Peter until Jimmy asked, "Aren't you going to open the present Santa Claus gave you?"

"Aren't I supposed to put it under the tree till Christmas morning?"

As soon as Jimmy heard Peter say, "Under a tree," he realized he had everything in his penthouse suite except a Christmas tree. Jimmy looked at Julie and said, "Darling, where can we get a Christmas tree?"

Julie was always on hand to solve Jimmy's domestic problems. "Let's get a bite to eat then we can go to Simpson's market. They have lots of splendid trees and lovely Christmas decorations."

The prospect of getting his first Christmas tree and then decorating it was beginning to excite the boy who had never experienced a family Christmas.

They finished their tasty dinner from the upscale Grape Vine Restaurant and Jimmy excused himself to make a phone call. After returning to the table, the preoccupied wheeler-dealer said, "Julie, why don't you and the wee man go shopping for a tree? I have some business to take care of."

Julie was no stranger to Jimmy's standard phrase. She had heard it often and would never question the handsome Glaswegian. She simply complied.

"Okay, Jimmy, but please, be careful."

He gave Julie an affectionate kiss on her forehead and pressed a large bundle of notes into her hand. "Buy the wee man the biggest tree in the shop and get plenty of the fancy lights for it."

Peter was new to all the proceedings but still looked forward to Christmas tree shopping with Julie.

Not long after Jimmy had left to take care of business, Julie sipped the last of her vintage red before saying, "Okay, my dear, let's go and get that tree. Remember to hold onto my hand because the traffic out there is busy, and we don't want to get run over."

Peter enjoyed the care Julie showed him and replied, "Okay, Julie, whatever you say."

Simpson's Market was a winter wonderland of toys, children's rides, and shelves full of candied apples and enough Christmas goodies to fill two floors. They also had their own version of Santa's grotto. This was completely different from the Christmases he had experienced in the orphanage where you were given a bar of chocolate, an apple, and an orange as a reward after enduring a two-hour-long midnight mass on your knees.

6

LIVE YOUR OWN DREAM. The alternative is to live someone else's or awaken from a nightmare of your own creation.

Jimmy arrived home after taking care of 'some business' and Julie already had Peter snug in bed. The wee man was asleep, dreaming of his first Christmas.

"Jimmy, what's wrong? You look as if you've just seen a ghost." Julie was more than a friend and was actually Jimmy's devoted lover.

"My darling, what I saw was worse than seeing a ghost. I saw a very good friend of mine hanging from the rafters of his bedroom."

"Why would he hang himself?" she asked, shocked at the thought of finding one's friend in such a state.

"Therein lies the problem. I don't think he did hang himself—I believe he was given some assistance in the procedure."

Julie uncorked a bottle of Burgundy and poured two sizable glasses. "What makes you think such a thing?"

"I'm no detective," replied Jimmy, "but I've been around enough situations to know when something doesn't look right. What I saw tonight was no suicide." He swallowed his wine in one gulp and described what he thought was a murder scene. "Julie, how in God's Holy name can a man tie his hands behind his back and then hang himself? No, this was a job."

"What do you mean, a job?"

Jimmy was reluctant to elaborate. "Let's just say my friend had some assistance."

Before she could make further inquiries, they heard a sleepy voice echo from the next room. "Is that you, Uncle Jimmy?"

He composed himself before answering. "Yes, wee man, I'll be there in one minute to tuck you in." He lowered his voice and said, "We'll talk about this later."

"Okay, my wee Scottish terrier," Jimmy said, pulling the covers up to Peter's chin. "It's time you were sleeping, but first let me give you a good old-fashioned Glasgow tuck-in."

Jimmy was still feeling overwhelmed after witnessing the tragic demise of his friend. He completely lost what remaining composure he had when the wee man said, in a very sleepy tone, "I love you, Uncle Jimmy."

He returned to his favorite easy chair with tears streaming down his cheeks.

Julie tried to comfort him. "I'm not sure what's going on, Jimmy. Whatever it is, I wish you'd tell me. Please stop doing what's making you uptight and anxious."

Jimmy cupped his face in his hands and said, "Julie, what happened to Charlie Green tonight will happen to me if I don't get out of the country. Please don't ask me to tell you why, because if I do, then you will be on their hit list as well."

Julie had always suspected Jimmy was up to nefarious deeds, but she'd never thought he was involved in a situation so dangerous that his life was in peril. She took into consideration that his demeanor was an act of self-preservation.

"In that case, I prefer that you not tell me what you're really up to—I don't want to know. Please just do whatever you have to do in order to be safe."

He then held his girl in his arms and said, "There's just one problem now, my darling. What are we going to do with that wee guy in the next room? You know I've become so attached that I can't abandon him. He's been rejected and left by the wayside all his life. My God, I know only too well how that feels."

Julie had also become fond of the charming child from Scotland. She was obviously thinking in a more level-headed manner than the man she felt so passionate about and said, "I've an idea. Why don't we get him set up in a boarding school? One of those places where the toffs send their kids. He's bright and will do well in a place like that. We both know he'll be treated much better than he was in that horrid orphanage."

Jimmy loved the idea but said, "That all sounds great, Julie, but what about the times when he's not in school. What then?"

She sat quietly, trying to think of an alternative plan but her thoughts were interrupted by a news bulletin on the television.

In his very proper BBC accent, the newscaster announced, "Tonight London has experienced multiple murders. A police spokesman at Scotland Yard suspects that it's drug related. There have been conflicts amongst the crime families throughout the city..." Before the newscaster completed his report, Jimmy switched the television off.

"Jimmy, do you think these murders are connected with the people who you suspect murdered Charlie...what's his name again?"

"Charlie, Charlie Green was his name and yes, I've no doubt who's involved in his murder. The odd thing is, Charlie was involved in lots of shady stuff, but he would never get mixed up with drugs. He used to tell me that if he got involved in that crap, it would be the death of him. Now, he's gone forever."

Then Julie said softly, "Jimmy, never once have I ever asked you what you do for a living. When we first met, you told me you were in stocks and trades. I wasn't sure what that meant but never questioned you about it." Julie sternly questioned her lover. "Jimmy, do you deal in drugs?"

"Absolutely not," he replied forcefully, "but I know a million people who do. I believe that those who killed Charlie thought I was part of the ring." Looking across at her, he added, "Darling, I have to take a wee holiday. I have a feeling I may be next on their list."

Julie's response sounded a bit self-serving. "What about me? What am I to do?"

Jimmy grabbed hold of the one woman he truly loved and said, "Wherever I go, I want you to come with me."

Her motherly instincts kicked in and she asked, "What about the wee man? He'll be all alone. He's only seven—just a child. What will become of him?"

Jimmy stared into space. "I'll have to work something out for him. I know a couple who could take him in. First, though, I'm going to make sure he gets the best Christmas of his wee life."

In the days leading up to Christmas, Jimmy and Julie took note of everything Peter hinted he would like Santa Claus to pull out of what was becoming a bottomless sack. Jolly Saint Nick would be the busiest man in the land. Christmas morning was beyond Peter's wildest dreams as Jimmy and Julie went over the top. The wee man's gifts were stacked five feet high around the tree. This was a day he would remember for the rest of his life.

Unfortunately for the young boy from Glasgow, the experience would never be repeated. The following day Jimmy broke the news to Peter that he and Julie would be going away on business. Peter would spend time outside the city with some friends of Jimmy's.

"Uncle Jimmy, can I come with you?" Peter begged. "I'll behave and do all the schoolwork Julie gives me, I promise."

Hearing Peter's pleas, Jimmy knew if he wanted to get out of the city alive he had to take a firm stance and ignore any objections from the wee man.

Peter would reside with Mr. and Mrs. Ralston in the small town of Lydd in Kent. At first, he felt his surroundings were strange—the transition had been abrupt. One minute he was living the good life in the center of the capital where traffic bustled and colors and sounds burst from every corner. Now he awakened to the sound of cockatoos, and cows mooing in the countryside.

The Ralston's were an elderly couple who'd had one son who had died from a rare form of cancer. Young Frank Ralston was like a brother to his friend Jimmy from Glasgow when the Ralston's first met him. They suspected he'd had a very difficult childhood but never questioned him about his past. They recognized there was a lot of good in him and he showed them tremendous respect. Frank's parents took to their son's young friend immediately and did all they could for him. Jimmy never forgot their generosity and repaid them ten-fold.

Peter didn't dislike the Ralston's and, in fact, after a short time began to enjoy his newfound habitat. However, it wasn't like living with his Uncle Jimmy in the hustle-bustle of London. As young as Peter was he subconsciously felt a connection with his flamboyant Scottish hero. He wanted to be like the man who showed so much affection and kindness towards him.

Prior to his departure, Jimmy gave Peter a long list of do's and don'ts. He promised he would be checking in on him from time to time. Unfortunately, that promise would not be kept. The Ralston's soon received a phone call from Jimmy's brokenhearted lover to say that he had died in a traffic accident.

Julie went on to explain without elaborating that there were suspicious circumstances surrounding the accident. In their effort to protect young Peter, the Ralston's thought it best not to tell him what had happened to his Uncle Jimmy.

After Peter was enrolled at the local school, the boy struggled to settle in. He was involved in many playground fistfights and was often accused of being the instigator in the conflicts. The biased teaching staff offered little sympathy when Peter tried to explain his side of the story.

Things came to a head when four boys set out to ambush the unsuspecting Peter as he made his way home from school. He was walking down a nearby country lane when they jumped out from behind a hedge. They gave the young Scott a beating and left him with a bloodied nose and two black eyes.

Mr. and Mrs. Ralston made their complaints to the head of the school, however their protests fell on deaf ears. Old Mr. Ralston was far from pleased with the outcome after speaking with the school principal and decided to take things into his own hands. As a former British amateur boxing champion, he gave young Peter a crash course on how to deliver a stiff right hook to the body and a left uppercut to the jaw.

It wasn't long before the wee man put his ring training into practice. He took on two of the four boys who'd beaten him up. He gave them more than equal to what they dished out. When the other two saw what happened to their accomplices, they decided it would be wise to befriend the young Glasgow featherweight champion-in-the-making.

7

SCOTTISH CREAM rises to the top after a bit of agitation and remains there.

Peter's relationships with his peers had its ups and downs, but he excelled in the arena of academics. For six consecutive years he was at the top of his class in all academic areas except mathematics. When he took a math exam it felt like déjà vu as he recalled his Uncle Jimmy's riddle: "If I had ten apples and you had…"

He was the smartest boy in the class and teachers who were initially reluctant to encourage the young Scot's talents were now exhorting him to further his education. As appealing as it might have sounded, Peter had other ideas about how to live his life. He wanted to emulate his Uncle Jimmy and get his hands on the quick buck. How he would achieve that, though, was still a mystery in search of an answer.

Throughout high school Peter had one friend who stuck by him through thick and thin and he made it a point to return the kindness and care that David Dubbs, or Dubbsy as he was known, showed towards him. They had shared a common background—shuttling back and forth from one foster home to another—and saw the world through the same looking glass.

Dubbsy's mother was a Lady of the Night, his father a merchant seaman from the West Indies. The seafaring father hadn't stayed long enough in port to witness the birth and

development of what would bec
dark-skinned David.

The boys also shared the sa
were both Leos and certainly wou

One sunny July afternoon a
the house, Dubbsy said, "Pet
things."

Before he could express h
him. "What kinds of things, Dubl

"Peter, if you'll give me a cha

Sucking on a blade of grass,
tell me."

"Why don't we start a busin
sort of business, let me tell you v
go to London and get a stall in
sell shit?"

"Sounds great, Dubbsy. Wh
mind?"

His friend squinted in the s
We can sell those new mobile ph
guy who has made a fortune sellir

Peter was quiet for a mome
entrepreneur, "Where do we get
you hope to sell?"

Dubbsy continued without
said he steals them. He's a profes
what I mean."

By now, Peter was getting
scheme. "Dubs, what the hell is a

Dubbsy thought Peter's ques

cket

six-foot-two, blue-eyed,

rthday, August 17. They
come leaders of men.
sat on the back lawn of
ve been thinking about

oughts, Peter interrupted

I'll tell you."
curious Scot said, "Okay,

Before you ask me what
my idea is. Why don't we
Petticoat Lane Market and

ind of shit did you have in

ght and said, "That's easy.
es everyone wants. I know a
hem."
and then asked the budding
e money to buy the phones

using. "My friend, Big Nick,
nal fingersmith, if you know

ritated with the hairbrained
ngersmith?"
on naive and smirked.

is and all I get is, 'Your uncle has gone away, and we don't know where he's gone or when he's coming back.'"

Dubbsy could see Peter was getting emotional and thought it best not to make any further inquiries. Just as the Glaswegian's longtime friend was about to change the subject, he saw an insect crawling through the grass and jumped to his feet.

"What's up, Dubbsy?" yelled the startled Peter.

"Did you see that giant creepy-crawly bastard coming right at me? I hate those things. Never ask me to go camping—I'd rather die first."

Peter laughed and then with a serious face said, "Okay, let's go talk to your mate Big Nick. I hope he's for real and not full of shit."

The boys took the train into the city to find out how the fingersmith had made his mini-fortune. Sunday morning was when the popular London tourist attraction, Petticoat Lane Market, sprang to life. The boys walked past stalls that sold everything imaginable, but what caught Peter's eye was not for sale. She was a pretty, young Chinese girl about the same age as the young Scott He had gone there on a reconnaissance mission but instead was distracted by the Chinese beauty.

The bold Peter approached the petite Asian and introduced himself. "Good morning, my name's Peter Cooney. You are the most beautiful girl I've ever seen in my life." Qualifying his chat-up line, he added, "…in the whole wide world."

The young Romeo was surprised to hear the girl respond in a polished English accent. "Thank you very much, sir, for your complimentary remark. Would you be interested in a new mobile phone?"

Peter displayed a sharp wit that was beyond his years and answered, "No, thank you. My partner and I are about to begin a business venture similar to the one you and your family operate. We're going to eliminate all our competition in this market and will eventually open a store in the city center. If I could please have your phone number, I'll contact you in the event an opportunity arises in our sales department. I feel your charm and stunning beauty would help sell anything."

The young girl smiled and graciously replied, "You are so kind, sir. I really appreciate your offer, however, I'd be unable to accept the position. I'm here to assist my parents for a few more weeks before I return to medical school to continue my training to become a heart surgeon."

She paused and smiled. "I have many years of study in front of me and I know precious little about hearts. However, what I do know is that you have a kind one."

Peter was blown away by the young lady. His heart pounding, he said, "I'd like to see you again. Could you tell me your name?"

The aspiring surgeon apologized. "Oh, how rude of me. Please, forgive me. My name is Charmaine."

"There is no need to apologize. I was remiss in failing to ask." Peter hoped the conversation would never end, but then heard his partner shout, "Peter, come on, Big Nick is over here."

The lovesick young Glaswegian shook the hand of his Asian princess and said, "Charmaine, one day I'll be holding your hand as we stroll through this market."

She said, "Peter, we never know what God has in store for us."

He made his way through the crowd toward Dubbsy and heard him yell again. "Peter, we're over here."

As he approached, his pal said, "I'd like to introduce you to my dear friend, Nicholas Stakis."

Peter looked Big Nick in the eye and said, "How you doin', Nicholas? It's good to meet you. Dubbsy told me so much about you." He smiled and added, "I hope only half of it's true."

The London-born Greek responded confidently. "Never mind the Nicholas shit—call me Nicky." He then suggested they go to a cafe where they could get a bit of peace and quiet to discuss business.

"Hi, Big Nick!" It seemed everyone they encountered in the market had a warm welcome for the wheeler-dealer.

The cockney shop owner yelled, "Will it be three of the usual, Gov?"

"Sure, mate, that would be fine," replied the Greek with the swagger of a Mediterranean pirate.

Big Nick got straight to the point. In a whisper, he opened the meeting. "Okay, boys, have I got an opportunity for you. Here's the deal. I get the merchandise—you know, the old dog and bones, 'the phones.' Many of them are hotter than a furnace and you boys get rid of them down at the market. We split the profits 50-50. That's the extent of it. Bob's your Uncle, we're making serious dough."

Between Big Nick's fast chat and his cockney slang, Peter was having a hard time keeping up with the Greek's proposal.

He asked, "Nick, I've no doubt that what you're proposing is fantastic. My partner and I will consider what you've said and get back to you."

Big Nick wasn't accustomed to being spoken to in such a manner. "What do you mean, you'll consider my proposal? This is a golden opportunity that will not be on the table after today."

Peter answered, "My friend, if the opportunity is gone, I'm sure there will be others for Dubbs and me."

Peter's partner couldn't believe the manner in which he was talking to the wheeler-dealer. Nobody ever spoke to Big Nick in such a fashion and lived to brag about it. The Greek was used to bullying people into submission and coming out on the winning side.

Nick stood. "Gentlemen, please excuse me. I'll leave you to discuss my proposition. I'd like an answer by five o'clock tonight."

Peter looked up. "Nick, thanks for the coffee but you won't be getting an answer tonight. In fact, it may be a while before we get back to you. However, if and when we do decide to go with your 'Golden Opportunity,' we'll be in touch."

Big Nick could hardly believe his ears and stormed out of the coffee shop.

8

BULLIES CHOOSE their victims and never seem to pick on anyone who they feel may retaliate.

It was quite an adventurous Sunday for the budding businessmen. However, very little business was discussed on their return journey to Kent. Both were preoccupied: one dwelled on thoughts of a Greek gangster, and the other was smitten by an Asian princess. It wasn't until they met the following day that Sunday was discussed.

Peter broke the ice. "Dubbsy, I've been giving your friend Nick's proposal a lot of thought."

Before Peter could finish, Dubbsy interrupted. "Peter, it really doesn't matter what you think of Big Nick and his proposal. He called me this morning saying his offer is no longer on the table. He said he wasn't comfortable doing business with my partner. He then added, if he sees either of us in Petticoat Lane, we're as good as dead."

Peter said, "Dubbsy, I really don't give a shit about that Greek bastard or his threats."

Dubbsy could see his friend was in no mood to be bullied or intimidated.

Peter's eyes flashed. "Fuck that big, greedy, greasy bastard. I'm going back up to the market next Sunday to see him. He isn't going to get in our way."

Dubbsy knew Peter had fortitude by the boat load, but he didn't expect his partner to take such a defiant stance. "Peter, maybe we should wait a few weeks to let things cool down."

Peter would hear none of it but did say he'd go alone since he didn't want Big Nick to be under the impression that the young Scot wasn't capable of facing him one-on-one. He was full of enthusiasm to embark on this business venture and suggested they copy what Nick the Greek did but do it better.

"Dubbsy, I've got it! Let's perfect the art of being fingersmiths. We'll practice till we can't be detected when we do the dipping."

"Do the dipping? What do you mean?"

Peter gave Dubbsy a you-can't-be-serious look and then explained. "That's what pickpockets call taking people's wallets and shit."

Dubbsy then made a legitimate point. "Peter, how and where are we going to practice?"

He had all the answers and replied, "That's easy. We'll practice on each other and if you feel me taking something from you, tell me immediately. If I feel you in *my* pocket, I'll stop you, too. We'll keep doing it until we are really good at it. Then we'll try our luck for real."

"Okay, Peter, you go first."

The guy with all the bright ideas stood next to his friend and pretended to bump into him, removing his house keys from his back pocket.

"Hurry up, do something."

"I've already lifted it."

"What do you mean?" Dubbsy asked.

Peter then waved his partner's house keys in front of him.

Dubbsy had not detected a thing but had the distinct feeling Peter had done this before. "How did you do that?" he asked admiringly.

Peter calmly explained. "Dubbs, when I was seven years old in the orphanage, I would watch some of the boys pick each other's pockets. It takes a lot of practice, but I think if we keep working at it we should achieve our objective."

Dubbsy was excited, "Okay, let me try it on you."

Peter stood and began to give his partner instructions. "Right, walk towards me and try to distract me."

"No need for that, mate." He waved Peter's wallet in front of him and now it was the instructor's turn to be surprised.

"How did you do that?"

"Wee man, when you bumped into me, I dipped you."

The two con artists began laughing. When their eyes met, they realized their plan now had the possibility of becoming reality.

Peter suggested, "Let's try to create other situations where we can work as a team. You distract them by asking them for directions or the time of day. This will divert their attention and give me time to work on them."

Dubbsy changed the subject for a minute. "Peter, are you sure you want to go see Big Nick by yourself? Why don't I go up to London with you? You can go talk to the Greek by yourself, but I'd like to have another look around the market to scout a good location where we can begin our work as professional fingersmiths."

Peter wanted to make sure he faced Big Nick alone but reluctantly agreed. "Okay, Dubbsy, I'll deal with our Greek friend; you scout the market."

They traveled to London in two seats that were at a distance from the other Sunday commuters and this gave them privacy to discuss and formulate their plans. The ticket inspector's voice echoed through the carriages. "Tickets, please. Tickets, please."

Peter flashed back to his first train journey to the once-unfamiliar city that he now knew better than his native Glasgow.

At the market, the boys went their separate ways and agreed to meet under the clock tower in two hours. Peter's first stop wasn't to find Big Nick but to search for his Asian princess. He wove his way past the numerous stalls and tried to recall where he'd first seen the young woman of his dreams. Spying a dark-haired young lady, he shouted excitedly, "Charmaine!"

The woman turned to see who was shouting and he was disappointed to see it was a girl from a different part of the world. He spent half an hour searching for her to no avail. He then decided it was time to look for the man who was threatening him and Dubbsy. He couldn't believe his eyes—the Chinese princess was having a chin wag with the Greek gangster.

He gave no thought to the possible consequences of disrupting their palaver. He approached and said, "Charmaine, how are you?"

To his delight, she remembered his name. "I'm very well, Peter."

The Greek responded brashly. "Mate, you're intruding on our conversation."

Charmaine promptly came to Peter's defense. "Of course, he's not. We've concluded our business and are finished talking," she replied in her usual polite manner. "It was pleasant speaking with you, sir. Please call on my parents' stall if you have need for a new or used mobile phone."

Peter asked Charmaine for the location of her parents' stall and said, "I have some unfinished business with this gentleman, so if you could excuse us for fifteen minutes, I'll call round to see you. I may need a new phone because there are so many stolen ones on the market these days. I'd hate to get one that was not legal."

As the young Asian walked away, Big Nick grabbed Peter by the lapels. "You're coming with me, you smart bastard." The Greek dragged the much shorter boy a short distance and then felt a jab of cold steel against his ribs.

"Okay, you big Greek bastard, let go."

The twelve-inch blade penetrated the man's thick skin and he released the Glaswegian, saying, "Alright, mate, everything's cool."

"You're right, everything's cool. You keep walking nice and slow or I'll stick this blade into your fucking heart."

They made their way toward the coffee house where Big Nick had first tried to negotiate terms that Peter found unfavorable.

"Okay, Nick, this will do fine. I'll be brief. I'm from Glasgow—it's not that big a place but what it does have is a lot of big-hearted people. My friend, some of those people reside in the city of London. I am telling you this to give you fair warning. If you threaten me or my partner again, you will be dead. It's as simple as that. In this market, I know at least thirty-five people who will do me a favor and take your life. If you think I'm bluffing, feel free to put it to the test. I don't mind dying as long as I know that I'm taking you with me. Now that you know the score, the ball's in your court, mate! Oh, and something else. Stay away from my Chinese friend."

During Peter's chat, the bully's eyes continued to scan the surrounding market from the window of the coffee shop hoping that one of his friends would come to his rescue. Fortunately for the little man with the knife who was playing the biggest bluff card of his life, Big Nick's reinforcements were nowhere in sight.

The meeting concluded with the bully acknowledging Peter's warning and informing him that he had set new boundaries in the market. "Okay, mate, perhaps there is room for both of us in Petticoat Lane. I'll not get in your patch but be a sport and leave some room for me to operate my business."

Peter was glad to hear the Greek's capitulation and shook his hand. "Well, my Turkish friend, I guess we have a deal." He was surprised as Nick shouted, "Don't you ever call me Turkish. I am Nichols Stakis and I am Greek. Both of my parents are proud citizens of the historic city of Athens."

Peter apologized immediately. "Okay, okay, Nick, you are a Greek. Remember everything that's been said, and you won't be a dead Greek."

They went their separate ways and Peter could not believe what he had just accomplished. He made his way back to where he had left his Chinese princess but was disappointed to see that the stall was cleared of its merchandise. The girl of his dreams was nowhere to be seen.

After checking the hour, he knew time was not his ally. He quickly made his way back to the clock tower to rendezvous with his partner in crime.

"Peter, what kept you?"

A glance at his watch proved he was only two minutes late. He smiled. "Dubbsy, what's two minutes between friends?"

"Peter, I've been putting the art of fingersmithing into practice and we're going home with more money than when we arrived." Like a nervous criminal, he darted a look around and said, "Let's get out of here."

9

FAINT-HEARTED KNIGHTS never win fair maidens, but slick-handed pickpockets always do.

Unlike their previous journey from the capital there was no shortage of conversation. For good measure, and as a result of Dubbsy's skillful fingers, there was a miraculous up-grade of their tickets to first class. With the extra leg room, Dubbsy was able to stretch out and said, "Oh, yes, Peter, this is the life. I could get used to this. Let's celebrate our profitable day and stop at Bernardi's for some of the delicious spaghetti everyone raves about.

"I would also suggest a nice bottle of house red to wash down the pasta."

Peter was enjoying Dubbsy's up-beat banter but was able to steer the conversation toward their future in the world of commerce. Putting on his leadership cap, he thought it was time to bring his partner down to earth. "Dubbsy, now that we have Big Nick out of our hair, what are your feelings about forging ahead with our venture?"

Dubbsy got caught up in the moment and said, "Sure, Peter, but can we first enjoy the fruits of today's pickings?"

Now directing the conversation, Peter said, "Of course, we can, but we can't get into the habit of blowing all our takings every time we make a few bob. Let's plan to build some reserves that will allow us to open our own stall and be real market traders."

Peter's pep talk brought the high-flying Dubbsy almost back to reality. "Okay, can we go to Bernardi's and discuss all the details over that delicious pasta?"

The more mature of the duo, smiled and said, "Absolutely, pal. I haven't eaten since breakfast."

They strode into the finest Italian restaurant in Kent where they were welcomed by the owner. "Buonasera, signori, bienvenuto."

Mr. Bernardi's English was almost non-existent, but he made every customer feel at home. He was welcoming them not just into his restaurant but into his great Italian heart. Roberto Bernardi was a talented chef, but his talents went beyond his culinary skills. He had a very melodic tenor voice and he would frequently entertain his customers with numerous Italian love songs from his extensive repertoire.

The young swindlers now had more money than they could have imagined and were shown to a table where they would have privacy. Dubbsy was full of the joys of life and reiterated what he had expressed on the train. No sooner had they ordered than the waiter brought two giant portions of the House Special, spaghetti and meatballs.

Peter unfolded the well-starched napkin and tried to reveal the game plan only to be interrupted once again.

"Oh, yes, Peter, this is the life." Without further ado, they buried their faces in their plates only surfacing for a mouthful of house red. When they finished, the dishwasher had an easy job because their plates were spotless.

"My God, that was the finest meal I've ever had."

Peter threw a napkin across the table at his partner and said, "You're wearing half of it on your chin."

Dubbsy quickly wiped his face. "Okay, boss man, now that we've eaten, let's talk business and see how we can make millions and enjoy meals like this every night."

Before Peter could begin to explain his plan, Mr. Bernardi's shadow fell over the table and he spoke in his pidgin English. "Okay, you boz a ready for a ma ice a da cream?"

In unison, the young businessmen with full bellies answered, "Oh, no thank you, sir. We are very full and satisfied. Thank you very much."

"Okay, but a give you a little liqueur on the house."

"Thank you so much."

Peter was now ready to reveal his master plan, ensuring that Dubbsy would eat in Mr. Bernardi's every night. More importantly, they were to become successful entrepreneurs. "Dubbsy, getting Big Nick out of the picture has opened the door for us. After all, we didn't need that big clown interfering in our business."

Dubbsy gave Peter a smile of appreciation. "No kidding. I don't know how you did it. I would've shit my pants had he grabbed and threatened me."

Peter brushed off the compliment and continued. "Okay, now that the Greek is history, we can concentrate on how to get a stall in Petticoat Lane. The first thing we have to establish is how much it will cost for a very small pitch, and then we can expand from there."

While Peter elaborated on the details of his plan, Dubbsy noticed a young, dark-haired beauty sitting at the next table.

"Dubbsy, are you listening to me?" Peter's stern reprimand refocused his partner's attention.

"Sure, mate, heard every word. You have my undivided attention. Please continue."

As enraptured as Dubbsy may have been with the young girl, Peter's talk about the prospect of great wealth took precedence. The more forward thinking of the two was now ready to lay out his plan. The ever-attentive waiter approached to inquire if they would care for anything else.

Peter asked, "Could I borrow a pen and a piece of paper?"

The waiter promptly returned with the items.

"Okay, Dubbsy, here's the way I see it. We're going to have short and long-term goals." He began drawing graphs and various lines on the restaurant's letterhead.

As hard as Dubbsy tried to follow what was being written, the happy-go-lucky fingersmith got lost in the details.

"Peter, can I interrupt you for just one minute?"

The architect of the elaborate scheme put his pen down and stopped sketching. He looked across the table and tried not to show frustration. "Yes, Dubbsy, what is it?"

"Peter, I just want to say two things. First of all, I don't have a flipping clue what all those lines and shit you're drawing mean. Secondly, I'm bursting for a pee."

Realizing his big pal wasn't the brightest light on the tree, Peter replied, "Okay, Dubbsy, go get your pee and I'll explain it to you again when you return. And by the way, don't forget to wash your hands and remove the spaghetti sauce from your chin."

While his friend was gone, he spent his time doodling on the letterhead. Suddenly, the girl Dubbsy had been admiring caught his eye. It was then he lost interest in doodling and began throwing a few affectionate glances in her direction. He noticed the young lady's napkin had fallen to the floor and he took advantage of this opportunity to show a little Glasgow chivalry.

"Excuse me, but your napkin must have fallen."

Just as he was about to hand it to the grateful diner, Dubbsy returned from the toilet. He quickly evaluated the situation and took a freshly starched napkin from another table. Reaching over Peter's shoulder, he said, "Here, it's better you have a fresh one than one that's been on the floor."

The pretty young maiden was enjoying all the attention she was receiving from the two frisky teens and thanked them. She turned to her parents and said, "Dad, why don't we give them some of my birthday cake?"

Peter smiled at his partner and within earshot of half the restaurant said, "What a coincidence, Dubbsy. I share the same birthday as…" He turned to the young woman. "Sorry, I didn't catch your name."

"I'm Erica and this is my Mum and Dad."

The rogues fell over each other trying shake Erica's hand and both said, "It's nice to meet you, Erica. We wish you a very happy birthday."

In an accent similar to Mr. Bernardi's, Erica's father invited the rascals to join them for a piece of his daughter's cake. Erica spoke to her parents in Italian but her new suitors had no idea what was being said and kept smiling. They had quickly become infatuated with the bilingual beauty.

She apologized for speaking in a language that she guessed the boys could not understand.

The smooth-talking Peter said, "My goodness, Erica, there's no need for apologies. My friend Dubbsy and I were just saying this afternoon how wonderful it would be to visit Italy."

Erica asked, "Which part of the country were you thinking of visiting?"

Before Peter could answer, the bold Dubbsy said, "The same part you're from."

"Oh, no," she replied, "I'm not from Italy. I was born in Kent, but as you can see both my parents are Italian and I've spent all my summers there."

"Where exactly are your parents from?" Peter asked.

Erica's mother had a better understanding of English than her husband and she answered, "We are from the southern part of Italy, south of Roma."

Dubbsy was feeling a bit left out of the conversation and chirped, "That's where Peter and I were thinking of going."

Then Peter laid on the charm. "Erica, with your parents' permission, I would love to continue our conversation. Would it be possible to have your telephone number?"

Erica's vigilant mother had been monitoring the situation and cleverly interrupted the flirting, saying in her broken English, "No, you not a get my daughter's number. But you give her you number and eef a she wanna talk to you, she a phone you."

Erica was embarrassed by her mother's reaction and apologized for her invasive intervention. "Please, Peter, may I have your telephone number?"

Turning to her mother she mouthed something in Italian that sounded less than respectful or complimentary.

The boys had enjoyed Erica's birthday cake and signaled each other to excuse themselves. As they were leaving, they once more expressed their good wishes for the birthday girl.

Just prior to leaving the restaurant, the proprietor looked at Dubbsy and said, "A Meester Curry, a think you a dropped your credit card in the bathroom."

At first Dubbsy had no idea what the Italian was talking about. He then remembered the name on the credit cards in the wallet he had skillfully picked—an unsuspecting William J Curry. He caught on to what Mr. Bernardi was saying and replied, "Oh, thank you so much, sir. Someone could have had a nice Italian dinner on my account."

The con men walked away from the eatery and Peter said, "Dubbsy, that was a close one. We'll have to be careful in the future. I think it would be best to get rid of the wallets immediately after the dip."

Realizing he had made the most basic of mistakes, Dubbsy agreed. "You're right. I'll never do that again."

10

WHEN THE GLASS *is half full, thirst never exists.*

Peter and Dubbsy always ensured their Thursday mornings were free so they could plan the weekend ahead.

Mulling over the previous weekend's exploits, Peter hoped Dubbsy hadn't taken his advice and destroyed the contents of the latest snatch. He waited patiently for his accomplice to arrive, well aware that he wasn't the most punctual member of society.

Passing the time, he occupied himself scribbling memos regarding matters to be discussed at their meeting. He was twenty minutes into his note taking before his friend arrived. Peter wasn't surprised at Dubbsy's tardiness as he had never been on time for any of their previous meetings.

He always had an excuse for his delay—he could be the author of the upcoming book entitled, "Reasons for Being Late." He entered with a ruddy face and breathlessly said, "You'll never guess what happened!"

Before he could deliver another excuse for his late coming, Peter interrupted. "Dubbsy, do you still have Mr. what's-his-name's wallet?"

"You mean Mr. William J. Curry?" He hesitated before divulging the wallet's whereabouts. He knew that if he answered, "Yes, I still have it," Peter may say, "I thought I asked you to get rid of it." On the other hand, if he answered no, Peter might say, "I was hoping you still had it."

He opted for honor amongst thieves and truthfully replied, "Yes, why? Was there something in it that you wanted?"

Relieved, Peter said, "Yes, I have an idea."

"What is it?"

"I remember the Italian calling you Mr. Curry, since that was the name on the credit card you dropped in his restaurant."

Dubbsy nodded.

"If I'm not mistaken, just as we entered the market I remember seeing a large electronics store and the name on the awning was *William J. Curry's Electronics and Mobile Phones.*"

Dubbsy reached into his inside jacket pocket and removed a business card from the wallet. "Yes, that's our guy, William J. Curry Electronics."

Anxious to share his idea, Peter said, "What we'll do is pay our good friend Mr. Curry a visit. We'll play the good guys and return his wallet with all its contents with the exception of two hundred and seventy-five pounds."

Dubbsy corrected his partner. "Peter, it was two hundred and seventy-eight pounds." He nervously wiped his nose and went into self-preservation mode. "Peter, if I return the wallet, Mr. Curry may recognize me as the one who dipped him in the market."

Peter smiled confidently. "Dubbsy, my man, that's no problem! Like the upstanding citizen that I am, I'll return Curry's wallet and tell him I found it on that patch of grass behind the bus stop just outside the market. If he becomes inquisitive, I'll just say I found it, checked inside for identification, and saw his business card and credit cards. I'll say I wanted to return the wallet to him personally."

Peter could see Dubbsy was having difficulty following his logic so rather than explain the obvious a dozen times he thought it best to slow down and spoon feed him little by little.

Although Dubbsy struggled to follow Peter's train of thought, he did have a legitimate question for the schemer. "What if Curry asks why you didn't return his wallet immediately after finding it? He may also think you took the cash."

The man with all the answers replied, "Dubbsy, worry not. Don't you think I gave that a lot of consideration? I've got it covered. I'll tell him I was going to return it as soon as I found it..." Peter paused to find a plausible explanation that would put his partner's concerns at rest.

Impatient, Dubbsy interrupted the silence. "Yes, you're going to tell him what?"

Getting a little frustrated with his partner's interruption, he said, "If you'll give me a chance, I'll tell you." Taking a deep breath, he said, "Okay, this is what I'll say. I was going to hand it in to my local police station but then I recalled seeing his store outside the market. I then decided the next time I'm up in London I would return it to him in person."

Dubbsy listened to Peter's longwinded explanation and added doubtfully, "Do you think he'll buy your story?"

Peter nodded firmly. "Absolutely, he will. After all, I had no need to return it in the first place."

Playing devil's advocate, Dubbsy said, "Okay, let's say he believes you. What's next?"

With still more probing from the unconvinced Dubbsy, Peter thought for the sake of peace it would be better to reveal the total plot. "First of all, I hope our friend Mr. Curry is there when I go to see him. After returning his wallet, I'll say I'd like to be as successful as he is some day. You know, make him feel good about himself and all that kissing-ass stuff. I'll say I have a partner and we're thinking about opening our own stall in the market to sell mobile phones. I'll assure Mr. Curry that it's not our intention to compete with him, however, we hope to have a big store just like his someday. Again, that should feed his ego. Dubbsy, who doesn't like to be complimented?"

While exposing his detailed plan, Peter thumbed through the contents of Mr. Curry's wallet. "Dubbsy, I'm confident he'll buy our story."

They were aware that the money collected from Dubbsy's exploits the previous week was long since spent. They had only enough money for two single rail tickets to the capital. Their mode of transport for the return journey would hinge on their success at the busy market.

They were now familiar with the surroundings of Petticoat Lane and they each went their separate ways, agreeing to rendezvous under the clock at the entrance. Just before splitting, Peter reinforced the need and importance of being prompt. He was now set to deliver his well-rehearsed story to the proprietor of the large electronics store.

Meanwhile, Dubbsy went to work picking a pocket or two. He worked the crowd of unsuspecting marks and was mindful that his partner's endeavor to convince the proprietor of Curry's electronics that he was an upright citizen would be crucial to their game plan.

On entering Curry's store, Peter was surprised to see the amount of merchandise on display. As he took it all in, he was approached by a well-dressed sales assistant with a polished and well-mannered air. "Can I be of assistance, sir?"

The ever-cool operator replied, "Yes, as a matter of fact you can. I'd like to speak to the owner of the store please—a Mr. William J. Curry."

The salesman judged the book by its cover and, taking one look at Peter's casual attire, replied, "I'm not sure if Mr. Curry is available, sir."

The confident pickpocket looked the assistant in the eye and countered, "Well, my good man, could you please go find someone who is sure? I have a busy day ahead of me."

The salesman was not amused by Peter's cocky attitude and became less respectful, dropping his polite tone. He leaned close and whispered, "Listen, arse-hole, get out of the store before I throw you out."

While Peter was receiving the salesman's harsh reprimand, he took advantage of the man's nearness and delicately put his skillful fingers into the assistant's hip pocket, removing the wallet. He then replied, "Sir, I don't know what position you hold in Curry's Electronics, but you can be assured that after I speak with the owner, you will no longer be employed."

The salesman was shocked to hear Peter's forthrightness and was about to manhandle the young upstart when the shop owner walked towards them. The irate salesman first acknowledged his boss and said, "Good morning, Mr. Curry, this person informed me that he would like a word with you. I have no idea as to the nature of his business."

Peter ignored the salesman's less-than-polite introduction and spoke directly to the store owner. "Yes, Mr. Curry, if you don't mind I would like a quick word. This is regarding an item I found that I think belongs to you."

Mr. Curry immediately knew Peter was referring to his missing wallet. "That will be all, Mr. Jackson. I'll take care of the young gentleman."

Peter followed him to his office and as he turned around he gave Jackson a sarcastic smirk. They entered the plush upper level of the office suites. Mr. Curry offered Peter a chair and asked if he'd like a cup of tea or coffee.

Peter politely declined. "Oh, no, thank you, Mr. Curry, but it's very kind of you to offer."

The store owner got straight to the point, saying presumptuously, "Okay, young man let's get down to business. What do you have for me?"

Peter was caught off guard, as he didn't expect the victim of the dip to be so brash. "Well, Mr. Curry, first let me tell you what happened. I was in Petticoat Lane Market last Sunday and as I was making my way home I found…" He reached into his inside jacket pocket and tossed Mr. Curry's wallet on his desk. "I found this on the stretch of grass just outside the market next to the bus stop."

The store owner quickly scanned the wallet to see what was missing before he replied. "As far as I can see, there's nothing missing except a few pounds. I'm very grateful to you, young man. I thank you very much." As expected, he asked the next big question. "May I ask your name, son?"

"Peter Cooney, sir," he responded politely.

"Well, Peter, why didn't you return the wallet when you first found it? Why did it take you a week to come and see me?"

The pickpocket, who had been anticipating Mr. Curry's question, replied in a very meek and well-rehearsed voice. "Well, sir, I just heard you say there was money missing from your wallet. I've no idea about any money but I'm returning the wallet as I found it. The reason I didn't come to see you sooner was that I didn't realize your store was so close to this market. Had I known this was your store, I would've had your wallet here long before now. Furthermore, it was my intention to hand it in to the local police station. But then a friend told me that your store was near Petticoat Lane Market.

"It has taken me a week to gather the money for the train fare in order to return it. If I'd had the funds, I would've been here sooner."

The man behind the large walnut desk was buying into Peter's story, hook line and sinker. He was so impressed by the young crook that he offered him a position as a sales assistant.

Remembering his lines, Peter said, "Sir, thank you for the job offer, but I did not come all this way hoping to obtain work. Besides, my friend I hope to save enough money and get a space in the market where we can build our business and, more importantly, our future. Perhaps one day we'll be as successful as you."

Mr. Curry had never met a young person with such drive and ambition. The store owner looked at Peter and said, "This is what I'm going to do for you, Peter. I have a dear friend and his name is Dave Goldberg. He owns a large part of the market. I'll have a word with him and get you and your friend set up with your own stall. Since you have been so honest with me, I'm going to cover your rent for the first year of trading, but after that, you're on your own." He then reached across his desk and shook Peter's hand. "Deal?"

For just a second Peter hesitated and was gob smacked with Mr. Curry's kindness—the guilt associated with his conniving action was eating at his conscience. Knowing, however, that there was no time for sentiment, he responded to Mr. Curry's philanthropic gesture by shaking his hand. "Deal!"

Peter thanked the generous shop owner profusely then said, "Mr. Curry, I'm absolutely blown away by your kindness and generosity. You are a gentleman, sir, and I thank you from the bottom of my Glasgow heart."

Curry smiled. "No, young man, I must say that I'm blown away with your honesty and integrity. Peter, before you go, is there anything else I can do for you? Anything, you just name it."

Without hesitation, Peter said, "Yes, as a matter of fact, there is something I would like, Mr. Curry, and I hope you don't think I'm being presumptuous." He cleared his throat and said, "That sales assistant that introduced us...I don't remember his name..."

"Do you mean Jackson?"

Peter nodded and said, "Yes, Mr. Jackson. I hope you don't mind me saying, but I'm not sure if that man is the person you want representing your company." He was surprised at the proprietor's response.

"For your tender age, you are an excellent judge of character. I've had many complaints about that man. I promise you that today will be his last day as an employee here."

Peter once again shook Mr. Curry's hand and made his way out of the store. As fate would have it, Jackson stood by the exit door and commented to Peter as he left, "Don't you ever come back!"

With his head in the clouds, Peter gruffly replied, "Oh, I'll be back, don't doubt that, my friend, but I won't be seeing you here."

11

YOU CAN'T *buy respect!*

The ever-punctual Peter waited at the prearranged meeting point and was now wishing he had read the weather forecast and worn a heavy coat. He was beginning to feel the ill effects of another wintry London evening.

Hearing the melodic chimes of the market's Victorian timepiece indicating it was exactly 5:30 p.m., negative thoughts fed his suspicious mind. "He's going to be late. He's going to be late. I just know it. He's going to be late." No sooner had the indelible thought spilled like errant ink, his partner emerged from the droves of people exiting the market.

"Okay, Peter, let's get out of here before I'm recognized."

Peter could see the anxiety written all over his friend's face. "Alright, let's go."

The two crooks hurriedly made their way toward the busy underground station, unusually devoid of conversation, only asking each other if everything had gone as planned. The answer was a unanimous yes.

As they entered the station, Peter asked the all-important question. "Dubbsy, do you have any cash?"

Mirroring his partner's cockiness, Dubbsy said, "Absolutely, I do. It's been a good day at the office, if you know what I mean. I have about eight hundred big ones."

Peter thought his ears were deceiving him. "My God, how did you do it?"

Dubbsy grinned. "I'll tell you later, but right now there's two cops over there so let's keep moving. I think they're on to us."

No sooner had Dubbsy expressed his observation than the policemen started to make their way in the direction of the suspicious-looking youths.

Thinking it wasn't a good time to be hanging around, Peter said, "Dubs, they're coming over. If we don't get moving, we're dead meat."

Without hesitation, the suspects headed straight for the exit that led toward the nearby bus terminal. Seeing the London transport authority red double-decker pulling away and picking up speed, Dubbsy managed to climb aboard. Then, holding onto the center pole, he grabbed Peter's arm and pulled him onto the open platform.

The bobbies gave up pursuit after seeing the shady characters disappear into the night. Both nearing retirement, the men in uniform thought it best to phone for backup, as it would be a better option than risking a heart attack. Being on the beat for more than the combined ages of the two they were endeavoring to apprehend, they knew that their fellow officers would halt the bus as it made its way toward the city center and capture the ones that were up to no good.

However, the street-savvy thieves were a step ahead. Instead of taking advantage of public transport as a means of escape, they jumped from the bus as it slowed to negotiate a sharp bend.

Peter caught his breath and blurted, "My God, Dubbsy, that was a close one!"

Still in shock from the unexpected activity, his friend could only mutter, "Let's get out of here and find a place where we can stay the night."

Peter reminded his partner that the day's takings would have to be sufficient to cover a week's-worth of room and board.

"There's no shortage of cash, Peter," Dubbsy said with a smile.

It was agreed that they shouldn't hang around, opting for a hackney cab to London's dock lands as public transport was now too risky. As they searched for accommodations, one establishment caught their eye. It had a bar and restaurant and was full of dockworkers and merchant seamen. After a further survey of the premises, they decided they could blend in nicely with the crowd.

As the barman served their first drinks of the evening, Peter lifted his glass and said, "Dubbsy, before we share today's happy happenings, I'd like to propose a toast to our present good fortune and our future success."

They clinked their pint glasses and found a table that had just been vacated by a sailor and what looked like a lady of the evening. Waiting for the remnants of the previous diners' meals to be cleared away, they browsed the extensive menu and ordered the two largest steaks the house had on offer—with all the trimmings.

Dubbsy happily mumbled something with a mouth full of Aberdeen Angus steak. "Peter, my man, that was a close shave today!"

Before his partner responded, he ducked under the table and pretended to be picking up his napkin. While there, he whispered nervously, "Peter, there's two cops at the bar. I think they're making some sort of inquiries. The barman is shaking his head as if to say no."

Peter had also leaned over and reached for the napkin, keeping a low profile. After a moment, he looked across the room to see the police officers leaving the premises. "It's okay, Dubbsy, they've gone."

Both came out of hiding and returned to upright positions, continuing to enjoy their steaks. The fingersmiths were now feeling more relaxed and began trading stories of the day's exploits.

"Okay, Peter, what did our friend Mr. Curry say?"

Taking a piece of French bread and wiping what was left of the sauce from his steak dinner, he answered, "Dubbsy, Mr. Curry was a complete gentleman. But there was a sales assistant who was a total arse-hole and did all he could to prevent me from speaking to his boss." Peter reached into his pocket and pulled out the wallet belonging to the man who'd hassled him. Fingering through the contents he said. "I should've known better—ten miserable pounds and a photo of his wife and kids."

After further inspection, he said, "Wait a minute, what's this?" He pulled out a piece of crumpled paper and recognized a betting receipt from a London bookmaker. He browsed the betting slip then read it aloud to Dubbsy.

"I think our man Jackson has a little gambling problem. This betting slip indicates that he put £150 on a horse to win but it also says that the odds were fifty to one."

While Dubbsy struggled to calculate what the payout would be if the horse had won, Peter stared into space trying to do the mental arithmetic.

Dubbsy proved incapable of even coming close to working the numbers and said, "Peter, I hate when you start mumbling under your breath. I wish you would speak up so I can hear you. Please tell me what this fifty-to-one stuff means."

Peter had just finished the calculations and looked Dubbsy straight in the eye. "I'll tell you what it means—if it won, we stand to collect. £7500!"

Anxious to bring his friend back down to earth, Peter said, "Let's not get carried away. We don't know if the horse won. Perhaps it broke a leg or came in last."

No sooner had the pessimistic words left his mouth than he spotted the evening paper sitting on a nearby bar stool. "Wait a minute, Dubbsy. I'm going to check the racing results in the evening paper."

Dubbsy's eyes followed Peter over to the bar and could see the look of glee on his pal's face—he knew they were holding the winning ticket. The ticket holder staggered back to his seat and said, "Dubbsy, I need a drink. What's just happened is un-flipping-believable. First of all, Mr. Curry wants to set us up with a stall in the market and pay our rent for a year up front. Now we've come into this windfall."

Dubbsy played the devil's advocate and quizzed him. "Peter, do we know if we can cash the winning ticket that you dipped from the arse-hole's wallet? What's his name?"

Peter quickly responded, "Jackson! Yes, that's right, it's Jackson."

"Surely, by now he has gone to the police and reported his wallet stolen," Dubbsy said.

After hearing his pal's take on the situation, Peter began to have serious doubts if the winning ticket really held any value after all. Frowning, he said, "I've got an idea. Let's pay someone to collect the winnings for us and we'll offer them £500 for their trouble."

Dubbsy shook his head. "What makes you think they won't take off with the lot?"

Peter was now determined to find a solution and replied, "That won't be a problem. I think I know the very man that will do the job for us."

Dubbsy knew who Peter had in mind, so he didn't bother to ask. It was no other than the indefatigable Big Mick Quinn, a local Irishman who had spent more time in prison than both their ages combined. Old Mick had been involved in numerous robberies, commencing a life of crime at the tender age of twelve. His longest stretch was twenty-seven years, but he excused himself and escaped after five, living incognito ever since. The truth be known, Mick Quinn wasn't his baptismal name—no one knew his real name. It was believed that Mick couldn't even remember it as he had so many aliases.

Peter and Dubbsy knew Big Mick from the local YMCA since he was always hanging around and encouraging the local youth to avoid a life of crime, although he continued to be actively involved in illicit activity in one way or another, albeit in the most discreet terms.

After a good night's sleep and a hearty English breakfast, the boys decided against returning to Kent by train. Peter suggested the bus might be a better option since the railway stations would be on the lookout for two suspicious youths. The moment they returned to their home patch, they sought out Big Mick.

"Hi, boys, what are you two scoundrels up to these days?" the Irishman asked.

Peter casually replied, "Oh, nothing much—a wee bit of this and a wee bit of that, you know how it works, Mick. But we have a little predicament and we were hoping you could help us solve it."

Never one to beat about the bush, Mick responded slyly, "Are you still exercising those sticky fingers?" Rubbing his two fingers together, he smiled and pointed to the boys.

"That's part of our problem," answered Dubbsy.

Peter took over and interrupted his partner. "Mick, I dipped a guy up in London yesterday."

"Please," Mick responded, "don't tell me you were caught?"

In a less than humble tone, Peter responded, "Come on, Mick, you should know not to ask that. We're good at what we do—there's not a chance, my good man."

Peter went on to explain the circumstances of their good fortune and how they had landed a winning ticket worth a substantial amount of cash.

After hearing about the potential windfall, and being nobody's fool, Big Mick asked, "Do you think the guy whose wallet you stole suspects his pocket was picked? Or do you think he may feel he dropped it somewhere?"

Peter replied confidently, "I was the one who nicked it and he has no idea I took it."

Big Mick said, "Okay, if you're so sure it's a winner, why don't you just go to the bookie and collect the money?"

Dubbsy asked, "What if the bookie suspects it wasn't our ticket?"

Mick was in no mood to argue and said, "Ah, give me the effin' ticket and I'll take care of it. Remember, I work on commission. I charge ten percent and not a penny less."

Knowing it was more than the £500 that they originally were prepared to pay, they also knew if Big Mick took care of it all would be well.

"Okay, Mick, it's a deal. We'll go to the bookie with you just to make sure everything goes smoothly."

After hearing Peter's proposal, Mick handed the betting slip back and demanded rudely, "Cash it yourself. Either you do it my way or it's no fucking deal."

Aware they had to submit to the big Irishman's request or they would be holding a useless piece of paper, Dubbsy added his usual two cents. "Okay, we'll wait here, but don't reinvest our share of the takings on another horse. Bring the money out to us."

12

HONOR AMONGST *thieves is overrated and often non-existent.*

Big Mick was a man of integrity so, naturally, he collected the money on the winning horse and handed over the cash after deducting his standard ten-percent fee. Then he said to the boys, "Did either of you geniuses happen to notice what the name of the horse was?"

The pickpockets were more interested in the pay-out, so they let Mick's question dissipate like a faint mist over their heads.

The Irishman felt obligated to remind them. "It was called Pickpocket."

This ironic coincidence ensured that the boys had the available finances to proceed with their business plan. Their endeavors had grown larger in scale than they had first envisioned. Despite the lean times they had suffered—and that they never wanted to forget—this windfall didn't diminish their appetite to hustle and accumulate more.

Peter felt the time was right to approach Mr. W. Curry and remind him of his promise to set the two entrepreneurs up in Petticoat Lane Market. He had assigned himself the leadership role in this, too.

"Dubbsy, here's the plan."

He'd heard this phrase often, yet never tired of hearing it. He had one hundred percent trust in his childhood friend.

"We'll go see Mr. 'stinking rich' Curry to let him know we're ready to make the big move and join the marketeers of Petticoat Lane."

They entered Curry's Electronics with a bounce in their step, yet Peter couldn't believe his eyes. It was the dreaded sales assistant Jackson making his way towards him.

"You came back after all?" Peter asked boldly.

"Your eyes don't deceive you. But I must say I'm surprised to see *you* here! When I told Mr. Curry you stole my wallet, he felt so guilty for wanting to dismiss me that he promoted me to head of the mobile phone department."

Sounding surprised, Peter exclaimed, "Stole your wallet? What are you taking about?"

Jackson grabbed Peter by the collar and called store security. Whispering harshly, he said, "I'll tell you what I'm talking about, you little bastard. You've been caught red-handed on the shop video security system."

Dubbsy, who was standing behind the sales assistant, shouted, "You've got the wrong man! We've been framed."

Jackson turned to see who was yelling. As he turned, he let go of Peter's lapels and the two fingersmiths scampered out the store and raced down the crowded street.

"Keep going!" shouted Dubbsy. "Don't stop. I think they're gaining on us."

Out of breath, Peter said, "Let's split up. I'll see you in Kent."

The two dashed away in separate directions. This confused those who had been on their tail and, eventually, they lost sight of them in the bustling crowd.

Once back in their own neck of the woods, the boys arranged to meet for dinner at Bernardi's. By now, they were familiar clients, so after being greeted by the proprietor, they chose a table in the far corner. They had some serious talking to do.

Dubbsy ordered his favorite pasta and meatballs and Peter his perfect steak—then they got down to discussing their next move.

"Okay, Dubbsy, I take full responsibility for the mess in Curry's. I never thought the place might have closed circuit security cameras."

Dubbsy was trying to be as sympathetic as possible towards the man who had made the worst blunder of his young and eventful life. Smiling, he said, "Oh, Peter, remember, we all make mistakes. But that *was* a big one. I mean, that was a real *effin'* big one."

"Alright, Mr. Smart-arse," Peter said, sounding unusually meek, "I'll make it up to you."

"Okay, my man, what's next on the agenda?"

"Funny you should ask. I've been thinking that we can set up in the market but not use our real names. I was considering approaching Big Mick Quinn and asking him if he'd welcome the chance to make a few pounds working in the mobile telephone business."

"Then where would that leave us?" inquired the curious Dubbsy.

On a roll, Peter said, "We could become Big Mick's backers—his silent partners, if you will. We'll supply the merchandise, Big Mick moves it, and everybody's happy!"

After seeing two empty plates at their table the waiter approached. "Do you have room for dessert, gentlemen?"

Dubbsy said, "No, thank you. That was delicious and quite filling. Could you please bring us the bill?"

The next day Peter and Dubbsy made their way to Big Mick's watering hole—The Clock Bar. They were sure that's where they'd find their new Director of Sales.

"Don't tell me," Mick said, finishing off his pint, "you guys have another winner?"

The fast-talking Peter said, "As a matter of fact, we do. This time Providence has brought us an even bigger winner. Let's sit over by the window and we'll fill you in on the details."

Dubbsy ordered three pints of the local ale and the discussion began.

"Okay, Mick, we have a great deal for you! This is a chance in a lifetime. All you have to do is put on that Irish charm and, with your gift for blarney, you'll sell many mobile phones. Before you know it, you'll be a man of great wealth."

"I may have downed many pints, but I'm not daft," answered the gigantic Irishman. "Listen boys, I've been playing this game since before you were born. This sounds too good to be true. If you don't mind, I'd like to give you some words of advice. By the way, this is off the record and there'll be no charge." Big Mick's dictatorial attitude took the wind out of the pickpockets' sails. "Boys, why don't we just cool our jets and you can explain in precise detail exactly what you have in mind."

Big Mick was attempting to dictate the pace of the negotiations by putting the two whiz kids on the back foot.

Peter sat back and coolly and calmly sipped his pint, submitting to the Irishman's request. With less gusto and bravado, they went into detail about how they had run into trouble in Curry's Electronics. Also, how they'd had to make a quick getaway.

Mick suggested they lay low for a while. He went on to explain that if they were seen in the vicinity of the market, the jig may well be over for both of them for quite some time.

In his most innocent voice, Dubbsy asked, "What exactly are you implying when you say, 'for quite some time'?"

Without hesitation, Mick replied, "That would depend on the judge's mood. If he and his wife argue that morning, then you could be looking at quite a long stretch—five or six years in the slammer."

Peter listened intently to the man who was no stranger to a life behind bars. He knew better than to interrupt, attempting to ensure they continued to live a life of freedom.

"Now, boys, the first thing you need to know is that the game has changed slightly. Instead of considering *your* opportunity, I instead offer *you* the deal of all time."

The original masterminds were now sitting at attention like school kids receiving a scolding and lesson from their strictest teacher.

First things first, Big Mick ordered another three pints and continued with his own proposal. "This is how it's going to play out, pals. By the way, if I ever find out that you've not been one hundred percent with me..."

"One hundred per cent? What do you mean, one hundred percent, Mick?" asked Dubbsy.

Peter nudged his partner. "We've got to play this straight all the way."

Mick confirmed Peter's statement. "Yes, don't F with me, because the moment you do, you're dead meat."

Dubbsy began to wonder if he and his partner had been wise in approaching the crazy Irishman.

Big Mick downed half his pint in one gulp, burped, and said, "Aye, by God, that's the best of stuff. Now, where was I? Let's see, you want me to show up here in this market and sell knocked-off mobile phones. How can you expect me to be excited about the prospect of that? The two of you must think that my head has buttons up the back."

"No! No! Mick, we don't," replied Peter apologetically.

Upon hearing the contrition in Peter's tone, Mick said, "Okay, okay, I believe you. Let me tell you what I have in mind. Instead of setting up a market stall, why don't we shoot for the moon and get our own shop?"

"But…" blurted the promising students who were now attending Big Mick's Academy for Criminal Activities or BACA. They would soon be working on a master's degree in Street Smarts.

"Please, wait till I'm finished, then I'll take a few questions." This from a man who, over the course of his life, had had a colorful criminal career. Mick glanced at his Rolex and said, "My God, it's almost three o'clock and I've got to meet my mate, Pat, at six thirty in the city. Boys, for the sake of brevity, I'm going to make this as quick and painless as possible. I'll have a word with my connections in the city and see if we can get you set up with a proper store. Please remember that these guys don't mess around. Never think you can take them for a ride or they will take you for a long trip off a short pier."

Mick stood and said in a slurred Irish accent, "Jesus jumping Johnny, that was a good couple of pints. I'd better be on my way, so let's talk next week. That will give me time to have a wee look at some properties that may be suitable for our purposes."

The apprentice millionaires thanked the clever, fast-talking Irishman for his time and agreed to meet with him the following week.

They watched the pub door swing shut and then Dubbsy said, "Peter, what're we going to do?"

Peter looked puzzled with the situation since the meeting had gone in a totally different direction from the one he had envisioned. "I really don't know what to think. I don't believe our friend Mick has our best interests at heart, although he did show honesty in his handling of the money on the betting slip. But all that stuff he's saying sounds too good to be true. There's something eating at me, but I just can't put my finger on it."

Dubbsy was hanging onto every word. "Well, if you're not happy about what's going on, then neither am I."

"There's one thing Mick didn't mention," Peter said.

"What was that?"

"He never mentioned money! Sorry, he did—he spoke about *our* money. Not once did he ever mention using his own money or any word of other cash."

They spent a long and hectic week debating "should we or shouldn't we utilize the services of Mr. Michael Quinn."

The uncertainty reached the boiling point an hour before their scheduled meeting with their so-called mentor.

Peter said, "Dubbsy, I've never been so unsure of anything in my life. I just don't get it. I keep asking myself why Big Mick is so anxious to get involved with us." Nervously scratching his chin for a second, he continued, "It was my idea to approach him in the first place, but now we have to ask ourselves, 'why is he is so eager to be part of our operation?'"

The confusion was too much for Dubbsy. "Why don't we forget all this nonsense with setting up a shop and just spend our money?"

"When that money's gone," Peter said, "then what will we do?"

"That's easy!" Dubbsy exclaimed with a grin. "We'll just pick more pockets and spend whatever we make. We'll never be short of money as long as we keep doing what we do best."

13

IT IS SAID the truth hurts...but the person speaking it seldom feels the pain.

Indecision plagued the boys' minds, reminiscent of London's notorious thick wintery fog. As they went back and forth, discussing Mick's proposal, the brainstorming reached a climax with a unanimous decision. Big Mick Quinn wasn't to be the third leg on the tripod of Peter and Dubbsy's business empire. That being said, they thought it best to honor their commitment and meet him in The Clock Bar at the appointed hour.

Every time Peter entered the bar, he was fascinated by the leaded glass door and how it had never sustained any breakage over the years. Looking around, the boys were surprised not to see the Big Irishman propping up the bar. After a quick scan, it was obvious he was nowhere to be found.

To be really sure, they gave the place a further survey. Peter checked the old wall clock to make sure there was no tardiness on their part.

As he stared at the old timepiece wondering what Big Mick could've gotten up to, he was shocked to overhear Joe Rooney, the pub's proprietor of forty years, say the likable big Irishman had had the misfortune of falling in front of an oncoming train at the Victoria Street underground station the previous evening. Despite having spent the majority of his life in Kent, the barman's Cork accent had not diminished and was every bit as strong as Big Mick's Irish brogue.

The talkative Mr. Rooney—who had given the Blarney Stone more than one kiss prior to departing the Emerald Isle—continued his tale. "I heard the police were treating the incident as suspicious."

The pint puller did mention something that gave Peter and his pal cause for concern. Though the place wasn't very busy, Joe Rooney leaned over the old mahogany bar and quietly said, "There's something Mick told me that perhaps you and your pal should be conscious of."

Dubbsy was standing behind Peter and moved a bar stool to get within earshot to hear what else was being said. Rooney whispered his message in a low, throaty growl. "Mick said that should anything happened to him, I was to tell you boys not to have any dealings with the Fallon Brothers. He told me some of the crap they get up to—they're bad news."

Looking around his premises like a hawk in search of prey, he continued, "For what it's worth, I want you to know that I completely agree with him."

The man who had been offering the advice pretended to be preoccupied as he slowly wiped his alcohol-stained bar. Glancing across the room, he said in an even-harder-to-hear whisper, "Don't turn around, but they're sitting over by the back wall where Big Mick usually sat. If I were you, I would finish your pints and get off your mark."

Though not fully understanding all that was going on, Peter and Dubbsy realized the barman was for real. They could see the reflection of three rough-looking characters in the mirror that had hung behind the bar from the day the first pint had been served. They placed their empty glasses on the now-clean bar, took the barman's advice, and left the premises in a hurry.

As they walked away from Big Mick's watering hole, Dubbsy sounded frustrated. "Where to now, Peter?"

Equally annoyed at the unexpected turn of events, Peter said, "You know, Dubbsy, I really don't have a clue what to think, but I know one thing for sure, Big Mick was a good guy, after all. In the future, we'll have to be more selective who we consider doing business with and not take things at face value."

Dubbsy didn't understand everything that was being said, but nervously looked over his shoulder and replied, "I couldn't agree more."

Now well out of sight of The Clock Bar and the sinister individuals who occupied Big Mick's seat, Peter said, "Dubbsy, let's cross the road to Kate Devoy's and get a cup of tea. We need to talk over the situation."

Old Kate Devoy had opened her tea room at the end of the Second World War to help support her two sons who had lost their father to German machine gun fire at the historic Normandy Landing. Over the years, the tea room had become a favorite meeting place for the townsfolk.

After ordering two cups of black tea and Kate's irresistible gingerbread, Dubbsy said, "Peter, let's go someplace where no one knows us and lay low for a couple of weeks."

The discussion continued over three more cups of tea and a second order of gingerbread.

Suddenly, Peter said, "I've got an idea."

"No, not another one!"

Defensively, Peter said, "It's a good one this time."

"They're all good," his friend said sarcastically. "Okay, let's hear it—there's a first time for everything."

"Spain. Why don't we leave and go to Spain? Think about it! We could score big with the tourists. They all have tons of cash to spend on their holidays. We can relieve them of those heavy wallets and that'll be our earnings."

Frowning, Dubbsy said, "Peter, I've never been on a plane before and the very thought of it makes me want to shit my trousers."

"I've never been on a plane, either, and I'm not about to start."

"Then how are we going to get there?" Dubbsy's look of bewilderment showed how thoroughly confused he was.

By now, Peter was getting slightly irritated and answered the question with a question. "Have you ever seen it advertised in the travel agent's window: 'Take the train to Spain'? Well, that's exactly what we'll do! We'll take the train to Spain!"

"Do we need one of those things…you know, when you want to leave the country?"

"It's called a passport."

"Yes, that's it, a passport," Dubbsy echoed.

Peter went on to explain that there was a passport office in Kent and that he had a mate who worked there. "When you know the right people in the right places at the right time, it goes a long way."

By now, Peter was brimming with confidence.

Dubbsy kept the banter going. "I suppose you know three bullfighters, as well?"

Peter laughed loudly. "As a matter of fact, I do!"

***

The pickpockets disembarked from the first leg of their journey and wandered around Paris before boarding the overnight express to Barcelona. Walking through the busy Paris train station, hearing boarding times and announcements in French and various other European languages, Dubbsy said, "Peter, I need a bathroom. How do you say, 'Where is the bathroom?' in French'?"

Being preoccupied with an attractive traveler, the question floated over Peter's head. Rather than repeat his predicament, Dubbsy wandered off in search of relief. Not having a strong command of the *English* language, French was proving an even greater challenge. However, there's the old saying, "Where needs must, the devil drives." This proved to be the case.

The overnight journey took them to the golden sands of the Costa Brava's sun-drenched beach. The two inexperienced tourists immediately found accommodation and then enjoyed a swim in the deep-blue Mediterranean Sea.

Later, Dubbsy stretched out across the warm, white sand and murmured to his partner, "Mi amigo, this is a million lifetimes away from rainy Kent. I could get accustomed to this real fast."

Receiving no response, he glanced at his friend and found old habits didn't die fast. Peter was enamored by the droves of young ladies strolling along the water's edge in their skimpy bikinis.

"Peter, can you do me a favor? Please, for once, take your eyes off the girls and listen for a minute to what I'm saying."

Without turning his head and looking over his knock-off polarized designer sunglasses, Peter said, "Oh, I hear you perfectly well, my friend, but I don't want to let this work of art out of my sight."

Four days into their vacation, they began to plan their activities for the remainder of their time in sunny Spain.

By now, the scorching sun was beginning to cause considerable discomfort on their pale and reddened bodies. To protect themselves, they had breakfast in a shadier part of the hotel grounds.

As much as they were enjoying the life of a tourist, they were beginning to realize the winnings from Jackson's bet were fast disappearing. It was time to get back to work.

Normally, Dubbsy was quite content to be led, but this time he had a plan to make things happen. "Okay, Peter, you've been the leader and led us well up until this point and for the most part you've done a fine job. But I've got a plan I think you may like."

Due to the acute pain of sunburn, Peter wasn't in the frame of mind to put up an argument. Giving his pal an opportunity to lead, he chose to adopt a 'let's give it a go' attitude.

Browsing over the pictures in the Spanish morning newspaper, he took another sip of his strong coffee and said, "Okay, Dubbsy, let's hear it."

Getting no response, he turned to see his pal dozing in his chair.

"Hey, Dubbs, are you alright?"

Jerking awake, he said, "Oh…yeah. I'm just a little tired. I didn't sleep well last night with this bloody sunburn all over my body."

"Okay, let me hear your plan."

"Oh, yes, the plan! Here's my idea. Why don't we forgo our return to Kent for another month or so and get serious with what we do best? Picking pockets! We can't do shit during the day because, as you've no doubt observed, no one is wearing anything to steal. We can't even pick shit out of their asses."

Peter was about to take a bite of his toasted French bread. "Oh, what a thing to say, Dubbsy. That's so dirty, but you do have a point."

Dubbsy was on a roll and continued to expound on his plan. "We can work at night in the bars and clubs. I was looking at one of those maps…you know, the ones they give to the tourists…and guess what? There are a lot of towns all up and down this coast. Why don't we work on one town at a time? We can make our way up towards the South of France and hop on the train and head back home."

Peter was so impressed by Dubbsy's knowledge of the Spanish coast that he totally forgot about the pain of the sunburn. He agreed that the plan was a good idea and said, "Let's start tonight."

"Not so fast, amigo! Let's have a look around first so we can work out a plan of attack."

The fingersmiths dressed for a night on the town and were ready for the reconnaissance mission. Initially, they opted for a more upscale establishment where they posed as two young London art dealers. They were confident the ploy would work, especially with the ladies.

They decided Dubbsy would play the role of the silent, confident one, and Peter the fast-talking flamboyant member of the duo.

After a few drinks in an upmarket club which was in the basement of the town's only five-star hotel, Dubbsy had to remind Peter of the purpose of their visit. Playing the part of the quiet introvert, Dubbsy wasn't comfortable hearing Peter talk all about his art collection. It became obvious that he was more attracted to the sun-bronzed female clientele than their wallets and purses.

"Peter, I need word with you." Dubbsy shouted to get his partner's attention over the scream from the DJ's amplification.

"What's up, bro?"

Angry, Dubbsy replied, "Don't give me that 'bro' shit. Keep that for your fellow prisoners, since that's where you're going to end up if you don't watch your big mouth."

Peter seldom heard Dubbsy sound angry and suggested they go outside to talk. In a jovial mood, the talkative partner showed the effects of the house sangria and said, "Hey, what's wrong, pal? Are you not having a good time with those beautiful ladies?"

"Peter, let's go home. We're not here for a beautiful time, or for the beautiful ladies. Remember the plan. I think we should leave now before you blow our cover."

Listening to Dubbsy, Peter realized he was jeopardizing the operation and apologized to his sober partner. "Okay, Dubbsy, you're right. Let's get some sleep and talk about it in the morning."

When Peter staggered, Dubbsy took his arm and led him back to their less-than-affluent hotel. Here, there would be no chance of any of their plans escaping from loose lips and revealing their bag of tricks.

Half of the act was up bright and early enjoying Ricardo's coffee and toasted French bread.

Unfortunately, Peter was nursing the severe effects of a headache that could only be attributed to the consumption of too much of the previous night's complimentary sangria.

"Good morning, bro!" Dubbsy enthusiastically and sarcastically greeted the man who looked as if he hadn't slept for four days.

"Not so loud. Keep your voice down, please," Peter answered in a somber tone. "I feel like shit and my head is ready to explode."

Dubbsy wanted to remind his partner how close he'd come to letting the cat out of the bag the night before. "I thought your mouth was going to explode last night. You were going fast at it. That's why I had to get you out of there as quickly as possible."

"I know. I'm really sorry I messed up and, believe me, it won't happen again."

"Peter, we've been friends for as long as both of us can remember, but our friendship will come to an abrupt end if there's any more of that shit." He looked at Peter and his heart softened. "Okay, let's forget it and get down to business."

14

FORTUNE FAVORS the bold.

Having settled their differences, Peter's and Dubbsy's concentration now was to pick every pocket on the west coast of Spain. Both agreed no more alcohol would be consumed during working hours, but they would have no problem toasting in the celebration of a successful removal.

Now familiar with the area, they returned to the five-star nightclub and since it was a national holiday, the place was bustling. This was also where the well-to-do locals in the resort town came to party. Playing the numbers game, it furthered their chances to—in Peter's jargon—'make some serious coin.'

The plan was set. They would survey a group that was not exactly scratching for their next crust. Peter would entertain them with his fast-talking humor and favorite card trick. While diverting their attention with his sleight-of-hand, performing the three-card Monty, Dubbsy had the opportunity to dip and collect from the unsuspecting victims.

With the combination of loud music, dim lights, and Peter's stand-up routine, it all fell into place. It only took the pair thirteen minutes to collect and get out of the building without arousing suspicion of any wrongdoing.

Their success was mainly due to keeping it strictly business and not tasting the free-flowing sangria, and all the pre-planning now paid handsome dividends. The evening proved to be a great success and the following morning they boarded the early train up the Mediterranean coast to their next port-of-call.

Knowing by holding steadfast to their well-rehearsed scheme, the master thieves were confident they could achieve the same success on other gullible groups of affluent tourists.

As the steam locomotive rolled along, Peter thumbed through his little Spanish phrase book, thinking he would put Dubbsy's Spanish to the test. However, his traveling companion was more interested in the rugged coastal scenery than in dealing with Spanish tongue-twisters.

The mood changed when Peter noticed two uniformed policemen walking through the train checking ID's and passports. He made a bold move and walked toward the officers to use the restroom.

As he passed them by, he overheard one of them speaking broken English, explaining to a passenger that they had been alerted that two thieves were very active in the region. They were robbing tourists of their wallets and personal effects in bars and nightclubs. Hearing the conversation, Peter made his way back to his seat.

"Dubbsy, let's get off at the next station. Hopefully, we reach it before the cops reach us. It doesn't matter where the hell we are, we just have to get away from these guys. They may have a description of us."

Lady Luck was on the side of the anxious thieves. No sooner had Peter informed his pal of the rearranged plan than the train stopped at a sleepy coastal town and they disembarked undetected. Walking down the narrow streets of a little fishing village, both agreed the place wouldn't be populated with the clientele they had in mind.

Nevertheless, they felt a sense of relief knowing the law was no longer on their trail. They decided to lay low for a few days before continuing the mission.

Sprawled out on the beach, they soaked up the Spanish sun and admired the Mediterranean scenery, mostly in the form of bronzed, scantily clad ladies in their bikinis. Intermittently, they were distracted by the odd fishing boats as they cut their engines and drifted into port with the catch of the day.

After their usual eight hours of relaxing in the sun and napping in their room to get out of the heat, they would grab a bite to eat, and head to their new favorite bar. It wasn't long before the likable duo befriended the charismatic proprietor Fernando. The cantina owner thought Peter and Dubbsy were different from his usual clientele and went to great lengths to have his curiosity satisfied as to why the new guys in town were dissimilar. In casual conversation, one of the many questions Fernando asked in his pidgin English, was what they did for a living. As their occupation was out of bounds, the boys remained tight-lipped and unceremoniously deflected the Spaniard's probing.

The few days they had planned to lay low fast became three weeks, and the now very suntanned Dubbsy began to get antsy.

"Peter, I think it's time to move on. We've done nothing but sit around and eat and drink since we got here. Our money won't last forever."

Adjusting his sunglasses to get a better view of a very attractive, young, bikini-clad brunette, Peter said, "I suppose you're right, but you must admit the scenery here is the best in the world."

"Well, hello, boys, I never expected to see you two in these parts."

Hearing an accent that certainly wasn't Spanish, both sat up from their beach siesta.

"I don't think we know you, mister…" Peter said.

"No, you don't know me," replied the stranger, "but I know you. You're the ones who ripped off Big Mick Quinn, then had him thrown in front of a train."

"What the hell are you talking about? Who the fuck are you, anyway? Get out of our sight!"

"I'll tell you who I am. I'm Pat Fallon and you two bastards will be seeing a lot more of me!" The sunburnt, crimson-faced stranger left, saying over his shoulder, "And don't think about returning to Kent—you're as good as dead if you do."

After hearing Fallon's threat, Dubbsy was in a state of shock. "Peter, what was that all about? Do think he's for real? Kent is the only place I know."

Peter sat quietly, thinking about the conversation they'd had with Joe Rooney, the owner of the Clock Bar. He recalled clearly when he'd quoted Big Mick: "Be careful of the Fallon brothers. They're bad news."

Composing himself and realizing Dubbsy was having difficulty handling Fallon's threat, Peter said, "Dubbs, here's what we're going to do. We're going to go look for that guy and talk to him. Don't you see, he's trying to terrorize us with his threats, but we'll give him a good dose of his own medicine."

Feeling a bit calmer, Dubbsy asked Peter how they could do that.

"For whatever reason, Fallon was trying to terrorize us…"

"Let me tell you, Peter, whatever he was trying to do, it worked! I was shitting myself when he was standing over us."

Peter defiantly said, "I'm going to look for the bastard, and when I find him, I'm going to give him a fuckin' big surprise."

After their day on the beach was interrupted by the unexpected and unwelcome guest, Peter suggested that Dubbsy stay in the hotel while he went in search of the man that was such a thorn in his side.

Dubbsy was reluctant to agree to the request, but after some discussion, acquiesced.

The fishing village only had two main streets with a handful of local bars. The pickpocket thought he would go from one cantina to the next in the hope he would eventually find Mr. Fallon. As fate would have it, the man dishing out the threats was found drinking alone in the second bar Peter visited.

"Good evening, Mr. Fallon," Peter said, walking up behind him at the bar. "I thought I'd come and have a drink with you."

Their eyes met in the long mirror hanging on the wall. Peter was the last man Fallon expected to see and having already downed a few, he slurred, "What the hell do you want?"

Very quietly, the boy said, "Mr. Fallon, it's not what I want, it's what I'm going to do. You see, this afternoon you behaved very badly towards me and my friend, and I'm going to punish you for such bad behavior."

As Fallon attempted to get up from his barstool, he felt Peter's gun probing his spine.

"Now, Mr. Fallon, don't do anything stupid or I'll blow your fuckin' peanut-sized brain away. If you think I'm bluffing, go ahead and put me to the test. However, as you can see, there's no one else in the bar. It's just you, me, and my good amigo Fernando."

Just as Peter gave Fallon these words of advice, Fernando walked over and locked the front door. "Okay, you piece of useless shit, tell me again what you plan to do to me and my friend."

Now on the receiving end of aggressive behavior, Fallon did everything in his power to get out of the situation. "Come on, son, I was just trying to frighten you boys, as my brother and I didn't want you working on our patch back home."

After hearing Fallon plead his case, Peter said, "I know your type—you're a bully. And like all bullies, you're very careful when choosing your victim." Now holding the pistol to the back of the man's head, Peter continued, "Mr. Fallon, I have a dilemma. If I don't get rid of you, chances are you won't rest till you even the score. But as foolish as it may be, I'm going let you off the hook. I may regret it, but I'll take the chance. But please know, if you ever try that stroke again, I really will kill you."

Fallon's complexion began to change upon hearing he was getting a reprieve, the circulation coming back into his face to expose the effects of the Spanish sun. Words of gratitude poured from his Irish tongue. "Listen, kid, I know I was out of order, but be assured you've seen the last of me."

For the time being, Peter was convinced the Irish bully was telling the truth. Unbeknownst to Fallon, though, as he spouted his words of contrition Peter deftly slipped a bunch of stolen credit cards into the Irishman's pocket.

Just as the loudmouth left the bar, two local policemen—Fernando's friend and his cousin—arrested Fallon. He was charged with being in possession of stolen property, mainly credit cards that were taken from patrons of a nightclub in a nearby town.

Having had a final glass of the house special with his amigo to celebrate a job well done, Peter thanked Fernando and made his way back to the hotel to let Dubbsy know the problem they had experienced with the Irish hooligan had been solved.

15

EVEN TO a blind person, all that glitters is not gold.

Hearing Peter's account of his run-in with Pat Fallon, Dubbsy asked, "Peter, where did you get the gun?"

The pickpocket laughingly responded, "You'll not believe this. As I was walking to Fernando's, I saw a kid's blackwater pistol lying on the street and I put in my pocket, thinking that one day it just might come in handy. Then, lo and behold, when I reached Fernando's, Fallon was sitting at the bar and, as they say, the rest is history."

So relieved that Fallon would no longer be after them, Dubbsy slept like a baby, and the following morning boarded the train singing the popular Spanish melody "Granada."

Although Peter had known Dubbsy since childhood, he never knew his friend had a passion for trains.

Sitting facing the engine as most train enthusiasts do, Dubbsy said, "Peter, the Spanish trains have a uniqueness about them."

Peter had no idea what Dubbsy was talking about, as he was just happy to be on the train without having to deal with intervention from the police.

His friend continued. "What makes them different from the British trains is the gage—it's different." Dubbsy realized Peter had no interest in what he had to say on the subject and reverted to taking in the beautiful scenery.

Meanwhile, with travel guide in hand, the planner was preoccupied with locating various coastal cities offering nightclubs that attracted wealthy, free-spirited party-goers. *Strike fast and move on*, he thought.

When the train that was bound for the Spanish frontier town of Port Bou was unexpectedly delayed at the tourist resort of Lorett de Mar, Peter surprised Dubbsy when he said, "Okay, I think this could be the place. I have a good feeling about it—let's get off and try our luck."

The happy-go-lucky Dubbsy agreed and followed his pal's intuition.

Walking through the town, they eventually found accommodations that suited their now-dwindling reserves. After a not-so-hearty or healthy lunch of burgers and fries, they began to search for a happy hunting ground.

Finding themselves on the main promenade, they were amazed to see the place saturated with ideal spots to put their sticky fingers to work.

Peter said, "Let's focus on the more upscale clubs for a couple of nights because, no doubt, that's where the top dollars will be hanging out."

"Sure, Peter, but I think this may be an area where we could hit two or three places on the same night—you know, the old double-take."

His friend agreed. "Okay, but it's essential that we have an exit strategy. Remember, as casual as police look, they don't waste time if something out of the ordinary takes place. There's no messing around. Did you happen to notice they walk around with Tommy guns? I don't think I could offer much resistance with my water pistol.

"They know the locals enjoy the tourist trade and will do everything in their power to preserve it."

Conscious their money was dwindling by the day, they didn't want to pay the exorbitant entrance fees to sniff around where they may eventually pounce. So, for their own entertainment, they opted for the lower-priced establishments to practice their Spanish with the locals.

Dubbsy couldn't help but note the pattern in his pal's behavior with the local girls—every time one gave him a second glance, he immediately fell in love.

This was confirmed when he overheard his partner's conversation with a beautiful girl. "My name is Pedro and I think you are absolutely adorable. I'd like to marry you."

No sooner had the words left his mouth than he was approached by a six-foot Spaniard—probably a fearless bullfighter. This particular matador spoke perfect English. "Pedro, allow me to introduce myself as the husband of the lady you want to marry. My name is Juan de Martinez."

The Spaniard put his massive hand on Peter's shoulder and lowered his voice. "My friend, I suggest if you want to live to see tomorrow, please leave her alone."

Without missing a beat and before Peter could respond, the confident local said, "There are many beautiful ladies here for you—in fact, you are so handsome you could have a different one every night of the week, but please keep in mind my wife is not one of them."

Dubbsy had witnessed the conversation and pulled Peter aside, laughing. "Pedro, it's not healthy to upset the locals. Let's go and get a quiet drink and stay clear of them. Remember, we're here to do a job and escape unnoticed—and more importantly, unharmed."

Peter took his partner's advice, and later said, "She wasn't that nice-looking anyway."

"I don't care if she was Miss-effin'-World, let's stay focused. Believe me, when we've got plenty of coin you'll have your pick of beautiful women."

The incident still rankled, and Peter's bravado asked, "Do you think I could've taken him?"

"Not a chance, Peter, the guy would have killed you. Besides, who gives a shit whether you could take him or not? You're here for the money, not his wife."

Peter was beginning to marvel at his partner's single-mindedness. "Dubbsy, I've never seen you so determined. What's come over you?"

"Well, I've been thinking a lot about Big Mick Quinn and what happened to him. You know, as much as I like trains, I don't want to end up being pushed in front of one. I think we should give it another year or so, and then start going straight."

Peter jostled through the crowded bar and, catching the bartender's eye, ordered another two beers. "You know, Dubbs, for as long as I can remember, I've been bobbing and weaving, ducking and diving, just to survive, and I've never given the future any thought."

Dubbsy could see a tear glistening in the corner of his pal's eye. "Peter, it's not time to give up yet. The future is always haunting us, but we should give it some thought. I think you're a great guy, but as you say, you've struggled all your life. Let's make some serious coin and get out of this business while we can. I seriously believe if we don't stop, sooner or later we're going to get nicked, and we'll be given some serious time."

After Dubbsy's pep talk, Peter found it difficult to sleep. The following morning, both were up bright and early to secure their sun loungers by the hotel pool where they could put the final details in place for the evening's snatch and quick get-away.

"Dubbs, did you happen to notice that big nightclub right on the beach?"

Dubbsy nodded. "Yes, and did you see the entrance fee marked on the marquee? It's more than a week's wages for the locals."

Peter was impressed by his pal's findings. "Yes, but we've got to speculate to accumulate, pal. I'm not worried about paying to get *into* the place. I'm more concerned about getting *out* after we do the business. I think instead of making a mad dash back to our hotel, we should bury our takings on the beach. By doing that, we, too, can file a complaint that we were robbery victims. With that approach, it'll alleviate any suspicion being directed towards us."

"Great idea, Peter!" Then, after thinking for a second, he attached a ribbon of doubt. "Wait a minute. If we bury our takings in the dark, there's no guarantee we'll find it when we return to pick it up."

"Dubbsy, Dubbsy, my good man, we're not going to the trouble of snatching stuff just to lose it. We can have a marker. It can't be obvious, though—you know, something very discreet."

Still expressing doubt, Dubbsy said, "Well, I'm going to leave that side of the business to you but do me a big favor! Please remember where it is."

Feeling the pressure, Peter was now beginning to doubt the strategy's wisdom.

The moment they arrived at the club, the plan was set in motion. First, they familiarized themselves with the layout of the place. Where were the emergency exits? Which passageways led to the beach? And once on the beach, where would be the best spot to bury their takings?

During this part of the operation they were conscience not to call undue attention to themselves. They knew it was essential to mingle with the crowd, as this was paramount if they wanted a successful outcome.

With the preliminary planning set in place, it was time for the fingersmiths to go to work. Peter gave Dubbsy the signal and they got down to doing what they did best.

Peter attracted a crowd at the far end of the busy bar, and Dubbsy slipped his delicate fingers into handbags and hip pockets. He even managed to snatch a wallet full of cash from one unsuspecting individual's inside jacket pocket.

Everything was going according to plan until a lady at the bar said to Peter, "Excuse me, don't I know you? Were you in the Dancing Matador nightclub down the coast two or three weeks ago?"

Peter decided to meet the question head on. "I've been in a lot of clubs in the past two or three weeks, but the Dancing Matador doesn't ring a bell. Besides, if you were there, I would've remembered—you're a very beautiful woman."

The attractive club-goer bought into the pickpocket's magical charm and lapped up his complimentary remarks. She then grabbed hold of him and whispered in his ear, "If you'd like, you can be my matador tonight."

As tempting as it was, Peter knew he had to stay focused. "I don't want to be your matador. I want to be your bull."

The blonde blushed at Peter's boldness. "Okay, my bull, I'll see you later. I can't wait to hold your big horns."

While all the sensual innuendo was taking place, Dubbsy was busy cleaning up. Looking up for a moment, he was impressed to see his partner slip his hand into the shoulder bag of the lady who was trying to entice him into her bullring.

Soon, they gave each other the signal that the party was over, and it was time to meet at the pre-appointed spot on the beach.

A few minutes later, they returned to the bar and could see there was quite a commotion and lots of angry voices. Suddenly, the music stopped, and the room was illuminated by the main house lights.

Several voices echoed, "I've been robbed!"

"My money's gone!"

"I've lost my wallet!"

"My purse is missing!"

Within minutes, police swarmed the premises.

Peter heard the blonde who, minutes earlier, was in search of a bullfighter was now searching for her purse.

He approached her and asked, "Has it happened to you, too?" Playing the game as planned, he said, "The bastards have taken my wallet and all I had is gone. I don't even have money to pay for my hotel."

The blonde—obviously head over heels with the charming Scot—offered the crook some comfort. "Oh, don't worry…what did you say your name was?"

In a broad Scottish accent, he replied, "Pedro de Sanesta." Then he apologized. "Sorry, how rude of me. I should've introduced myself. And no, I'm not a bullfighter. My father was from Mexico and my mother is Scottish, hence the Latino name."

The blonde introduced herself as Marlin Mullen.

"Don't worry, Pedro. My parents own an estate on the Costa Brava. You are welcome to come home with me—there are many bedrooms on the property."

Casually, Peter asked, "Are there any bullrings?"

With the house lights turned up, Peter could see Dubbsy was also in deep conversation with an attractive local.

He excused himself from his stunning beauty to use the restroom. Walking by his pal, he winked, and the two rogues met at the urinals. After a brief conversation, they decided it would be a good idea to go their separate ways and meet on the beach the following morning. By staying apart, it would strengthen their position that they weren't the nightclub pickpockets.

Returning to Marlin, Peter could see she was registering her complaint with local police.

"Are you okay, my dear?" he asked.

Showing as much concern as she was receiving, she said, "Oh, Pedro, if you've had something stolen, please tell this lovely police officer. He said they already caught one of the pickpockets who was operating in that club I was telling you about, The Dancing Matador." Slipping her arm through his, she added, "The nice policeman also said they have one of the pickpockets behind bars and he and his men will soon catch the rest of the thieves."

Peter suspected the trap he'd laid for Pat Fallon had worked perfectly, and he was taking the rap for Dubbsy and himself.

16

WAKING UP in luxurious surroundings, the man who'd begun life in an orphanage thought, "This is not a bull ring."

Then he heard three gentle taps on the bedroom door and the sultry voice of a female. "Are you awake, Pedro?"

Under his sleepy breath, he murmured, "Who the fuck is Pedro?"

Quickly gathering his thoughts, he replied, "Yes, just about. I'll be right there."

Splashing water on his face he couldn't believe his eyes—the view of the Mediterranean from the bathroom window was absolutely stunning. Yet an even better view awaited him on the other side of the bedroom door, the beautiful Marlin—the woman who offered shelter to the man who had supposedly suffered at the hands of the same pickpocket that had robbed her.

Taking his hand, she escorted him to meet her parents. She stopped before they entered the outside dining area and gave him a delicate kiss on his cheek.

"Mum, Dad, this is Pedro, the gentleman I was telling you about who I met in the club last night. He was also a victim to the pickpocket and lost his wallet."

In unison, Marlin's parents welcomed the young lodger. "Please, have a seat, Pedro, and join us for breakfast."

Hearing the kindness in Marlin's mother's tone, he felt he was dreaming. It seemed a million years since he'd been treated with such affection. He immediately thought of Jimmy, the man who had given him and Danny a roof over their heads when they first arrived in London.

Peter thanked Marlin's parents and tucked into a full English breakfast.

"What do you do back home, Pedro?" inquired Marlin's mother.

Again, Peter almost forget who Pedro was and then flowed into conversation.

"I'm a student, Mrs. Mullen. Well, I'm no longer a student... I've just graduated in electronics at Strathclyde University in Glasgow. As for the future, I'm interested in opening my own store selling mobile phones and electronic equipment. You know, high end music centers and computers."

While Peter mapped out his future for Marlin's mother and father, their daughter was mesmerized by his charm and good looks.

"Marlin, why don't you show your friend around the estate?" suggested the kind-hearted mother. "Do you like horses, Pedro?"

The quick-witted Glaswegian replied, "Only when they win, Mrs. Mullen."

Marlin's father almost choked with laughter at Peter's comeback. "You're a funny guy, Pedro—a man after my own heart. I've been known to invest in a bit of livestock myself, but the horses don't seem to try very hard when I bet on them."

Enjoying the breakfast table chatter, Peter said, "Mr. Mullen, as you no doubt have realized, there are no skinny bookmakers—the odds are always stacked in their favor."

The breakfast over, Mr. Mullen excused himself. Shaking Peter's hand, he said, "I enjoyed meeting you and hope to see more of you, but in the meantime, please excuse me. I have to call London—I've some business to take care of."

The very mannerly Peter stood from the table and thanked the estate owner and his wife for breakfast and their kindness.

Walking across the courtyard, Marlin said, "Pedro, you didn't really answer Mother's question. Do you like horses?"

The man being questioned sensed horses were a big part of Marlin's life and replied, "I like all animals except cats."

The young lady on his arm giggled. "I'm with you there. I'm not that fond of cats, either. I like dogs, but horses are my favorite."

Peter was curious as to why Marlin had asked about his affection for horses and said, "Why do you like horses so much? Do you do a lot of riding?"

"Yes, of course, I'm a member of the British Olympic show jumping team."

To himself, Peter thought, *My God, there's some serious money here.*

Looking at his watch, he said, "Oh, Marlin, I have to go. I need to explain to the hotel owner what happened to me in the club last night, as he'll be expecting to be paid."

"But you've no money, Pedro. Reaching into her pocket, she said, "Here, please take this. There's about five hundred pounds there—I hope it helps for the time being. I'll have our driver take you into town."

Peter could not believe what was happening. "I promise I'll return everything to you."

"I'm not sure what you mean by 'everything'. I've just given you some money. Don't worry about it, but please come back this evening. We can have dinner alone on the balcony. My parents have an engagement in town with a British diplomat."

***

With his limited Spanish, Peter knew he was running late and endeavored to encourage the Mullen's driver to keep his foot on the gas.

Seeing Dubbsy sitting on the beach close to where the takings were buried, he apologized for his tardiness. "Sorry I'm late, Dubbsy."

"My God, I thought you'd never show up," his partner responded in an irritated manner.

Defensively, Peter said, "Wait a minute. Cut me a bit of slack—you've been late since the first day we met."

All about business, Dubbsy said, "Do you remember the spot?"

"Sure, I do."

Dubbsy looked around and said, "Walk away. There are two cops up there watching us."

Peter strolled along the beach by the water's edge until he heard Dubbsy's signature whistle. "Okay, I think we're all clear. Let's get the gear and get out of here."

Peter saw the rock—the marker—and got to work shoveling the sand away with his hands. He was about three minutes into the dig when he retrieved the plastic bag with the loot. "Got it! Let's get back to the hotel. And by the by way, I've quite a story for you."

Dubbsy hadn't heard his partner sound so excited in a long time.

As they emptied the contents of the plastic bag, the bed amassed an assortment of credit cards and foreign currency. Peter suggested the credit cards be put to the side as they would have to be destroyed. "It's too risky to use the cards—they'd for sure link us to the crime."

"You know, Peter, I've never thought of our activity as being a crime. I guess we've been doing this for so long, it feels like second nature."

While Dubbsy was expressing his view on their occupation, Peter was engrossed in reading a letter that had been lying beside a bundle of cash.

"What's caught your eye?"

"Remember I was saying I had a story for you? Well, it's about the person this letter was written to."

Dubbsy stopped what he was doing to follow Peter's story. "Last night when we went our separate ways, I'm not sure where you ended up, but for me—I was in heaven."

Not to be outdone, Dubbsy boastfully said, "Oh, I was in heaven, too! Did you not see the ass that little Spaniard had? Peter, I'm telling you, she was quite a lady."

"I believe you, but let me tell you about my friend Marlin."

"Oh, man, this sounds serious. Please don't tell me you're in love again. Remember the deal, we're here for the money, not for the ladies."

"I know that, but this is different."

"No, no, they're all the same," Dubbsy argued. "Don't you go getting all soft on me!"

Peter said, "For God's sake, let me tell you what happened last night."

Lying across the other bed, Dubbsy took a deep breath. "Okay, let's hear it."

Peter went on to tell him his bed-and-breakfast experience, then said, "When I was giving Marlin the chat in the club, I took her purse from her bag and this letter was in it. It's addressed to her from some guy saying he's going to top himself if she doesn't marry him."

Expressing no emotion, Dubbsy said, "So what if the clown wants to do himself in? I say, let him go right ahead."

Peter sounded anxious. "That's fine, Dubbs, but he's saying he's going to kill her first."

Dubbsy stopped counting and threw the stack of notes back onto the bed. "Now that's different! Let's go and see the guy and talk a bit sense into him, if you know what I mean."

"That's easier said than done. He didn't exactly leave his home address on the letter."

Doing his best Sherlock Homes impersonation, Dubbsy said, "Well, my dear Watson, you'll have to go and see your friend...what's her name?"

Getting irritated with his pal's insincere attitude towards what he considered a very serious situation, Peter said, "Dubbsy, what is it with you? You can never remember any bastard's name. It's Marlin. Marlin! Now, do me a big favor and please don't be asking me ten minutes from now what her name is."

Dubbsy could see the woman meant a lot to his pal and said, "Okay, okay, I get it! Her name's Mary."

They started to laugh, and then Peter said, "Seriously, Dubbs, we have to get hold of this clown."

"I agree, Peter, but can we count the money first?"

Once the usable cash was separated from the cards and travelers checks and other trinkets, the pickpockets were back in business, having enough money to last them at least a year on the Spanish coast.

After splitting the earnings fifty-fifty and putting some by in what they referred to as their emergency reserve fund, Peter said, "The first thing I must do is return the five hundred pounds to Marlin."

Dubbsy reminded him, "Not a penny more or she may ask where you got so much money."

The ever-sharp Peter replied, "I'll just tell her I have a wealthy mate with a big heart."

Although no set time had been arranged for dinner, Peter thought he would surprise his date and show up earlier in case she wanted show him her horses—or better still, her bullring.

Stopping off at a small florist shop, he picked a dozen assorted roses, thinking, *This ought to get the party started.*

17

NEVER LOOK *a gift horse in the mouth.*

Driving past the large sign that hung over the freshly painted white gates on the approach to Marlin's parents' estate, Peter tried to figure out what "Bienvenido Granja de Paloma Blanca" meant. When he asked the taxi driver for an English translation, he was met by a blank stare—the driver's English was on a par with Peter's Spanish.

Now back in the money, the pickpocket paid the taxi fare and included a sizable tip. The driver checked the bundle of peseta notes and thought Peter's generosity may be due to his lack of understanding about how to count Spanish currency. Rather than question his passenger, he decided to make a quick exit from the premises—his wheels spun on the dry, sunbaked ground and created a cloud of dust that made the car invisible.

As he was brushing the dust from his clothes, Peter heard the clip-clop, clip-clop, of the resident equestrian champion.

"Buenas tardes, mi amigo. Cómo está?"

The guest apologized for not being able to respond in Spanish and answered, "Marlin, now that I see you, if I was doing any better it would be a mortal sin."

Not having been raised Catholic, the beauty on horseback didn't appreciate Peter's humor.

After she'd made a professional dismount from her sizable four-legged friend, Peter presented her with the dozen roses.

Kissing him smack on the lips, she said, "Thank you so much—you're sweet. I couldn't tell you the last time someone bought me flowers."

Laughing, Peter said, "Oh, I didn't buy them, I stole them from the garden next to my hotel."

"Not a chance! Pedro, I don't believe you're capable of stealing so much as a cookie from your mother's jar."

Peter was tempted to say, "You're wrong on two counts. Number one, I don't have a mother, and number two, I've been stealing my whole life," but thought better of it.

Marlin handed the reins to one of the stable hands then said to her date, "I didn't expect you so soon. Please let me get cleaned up for dinner. Feel free to explore the estate and I'll be ready soon."

She smiled sweetly and left him on his own.

Looking around, he didn't know where to start, but made his way toward the main building. There at the entrance to a long corridor, he noticed a wall of photographs of people who had visited the estate. Smack in the middle was Queen Elizabeth and her husband, the Duke of Edinburgh, surrounded by a host of London's well-to-do socialites. He also saw a number of his favorite music and sports personalities, including his Scottish soccer hero, Jimmy Johnstone of Glasgow Celtic.

Still browsing sometime later, he heard a voice behind him. "Well, Mr. Pedro Martinez, my Scottish matador, are you ready to dine?"

Once again forgetting his alias, he had to think twice to remember to whom the beautiful hostess was speaking. "Oh! Oh, yes. My goodness, you look so adorable. One minute you're riding a horse and the next minute," he pointed to the royal couple's photo, "you're dressed to dine with those two."

Taking the bemused Peter's hand, Marlin quietly whispered, "Who needs a duke when I have a bull?"

All the innuendo was beginning to whet the matador's appetite, but not for the contents of the kitchen.

As she led Peter to the outdoor terrace, he could hardly contain himself. "Marlin, I've never experienced anything like this. There must be a million candles on this table and the setting is absolutely unbelievable!"

He was becoming uncomfortable with the number of people catering to their needs. Taking Marlin's hand, he said, "I hope you don't mind me saying, but I feel like a bull in a china shop."

At hearing Peter's comment, Marlin burst into a fit of giggles, nearly knocking over her crystal glass of champagne. "Pedro, you're so funny. I would like you to know, if you've not already noticed, that I find you irresistible."

With a mouthful of chicken, Peter replied, "The feeling is moo-hull." Taking the embroidered napkin displaying the family crest, he swallowed, wiped his mouth and said, "Sorry, I mean mutual."

The couple could not have wished for a more perfect evening. However, as much as romance was in the air, Peter was preoccupied with the contents of the letter he had read to Dubbsy four hours earlier. The problem was, he had no way to broach the subject. After some contemplation, he thought he would take the delicate approach.

Holding the hand of the lady with whom he was quickly falling in love, he said, "Marlin, I have a question for you and I very much hope you don't mind if I ask it."

Giving the meal time to digest, they sat on a sofa that was strategically positioned so they could appreciate the stunning view of the bay.

Marlin snuggled against her dinner guest. "Pedro, ask me anything, but I'm not sure if I can give you the answer you're looking for."

Taking a deep breath, he said, "Well, here goes. Marlin, you're so attractive, and you have all these things and wealthy parents." Peter qualified his statement by saying, "You know, horses and stuff.

"What I was wondering is why don't you have a husband, or at least a steady boyfriend?"

Marlin sat upright and stared at her dinner date.

However, before she could verbalize her thoughts, Peter became aware that he'd hit a nerve. "Oh, please, don't get me wrong! I'm happy you don't have another man, and I'll tell you why." Holding her by the shoulders, he said, "I'm so in love with you, I can hardly breathe. Since the moment I set eyes on you, I couldn't believe my good fortune—and we get along so well."

Hearing the intimacy in the voice of the man she believed to be Pedro extinguished the fire from Marlin's thoughts, as she melted into the pickpocket's arms. Then she said, "Pedro, please tell me all about yourself."

Hearing the request, Peter almost froze. It was his intention to extract as much information as he could from the woman he was in love with and now the tables were being turned. "Oh, I'm just Mr. Steady Eddie. There's nothing too exciting about me. I studied for my exams and, thank God, received decent grades, and now I'm trying to put that education to work."

As humble as Peter tried to sound, somehow Marlin could see past the veneer of false humility. "No, Pedro, I'm not buying that story. Please, don't think of me as a stupid blonde—there is far more to you than meets the eye. For starters, I don't believe for a minute that you are one of the world's, as you put it,

'Steady Eddie's.' No, sir, you are a true fighter of bulls—in or outside the ring."

Peter was beginning to feel uncomfortable with the way the conversation was heading and thought it best to change the subject...and change it fast. "Marlin, how long have you been riding horses?"

The fresh topic was welcomed by the lady who seemed to live her life for the opportunity to ride and take care of her favorite animals.

"You know, I can't remember not being around horses. My parents love show jumping and I guess they always wanted me to be involved in the sport. I'm so grateful to them for raising me in such an environment."

She spoke for what felt like an eternity about horses and show jumping. It brought such a relief, as it steered the conversation away from the pickpocket's activities.

"Pedro, my parents won't be home tonight," she said softly. "Please stay with me."

The bold Peter was never going to refuse such an open invitation, especially from a wonderful lady. Throughout his life, he'd had many sleepless nights, but this was one he would cherish for a long time to come. He had never experienced such passion that could compare to the night he spent with Marlin Mullen.

He was awakened by the cock-a-doodle-doos of the farm's many feathered friends. Wiping the sleep from his eyes, he looked out to see his bed partner putting her horse through its paces in a circular fenced arena across from the main courtyard.

Showered and dressed, he met the girl of his dreams for breakfast in the hope they could have an encore of the previous evening's activities. He was disappointed when Marlin informed him she had some urgent business to take care of in London and would be flying out in the afternoon.

Agitated about her sudden change of plans, Peter asked, "What kind of business? We're just getting to know each other—can it not wait?"

Sensing Peter's concern, she said, "Honey, I need you to trust me on this. It's a matter of life and death."

"No, Marlin! I can't let you go alone. I want to go with you!" He felt her giving him the same strange look he had seen at dinner right before he'd changed the subject to horses and show jumping.

"Pedro, is there something you know about me that you're not telling?" Marlin replied in a suspicious and curious tone.

In a similar tone, he countered, "I'm not sure what you're talking about, but you don't sound very happy to be returning to London. I'm just wondering if you'd feel safer if I were with you." Peter knew using the word 'safer' might arouse more suspicion, but he had to play the hand he'd been dealt. Besides, this was the one woman he really cherished and was anxious to protect.

He was surprised when she started to cry. "Pedro you've no idea the mess I'm in."

"Marlin, my darling, I guess that makes two of us, because you've no idea the mess I'm in also."

Still crying, she said, "If you really knew the truth, you'd never speak to me again."

Peter held the woman he adored and said, "Listen, young lady, this conversation is getting very, very interesting, because something tells me we are both in the shit, albeit for different reasons." Although Peter had an idea what Marlin was going through, she was curious as to what Pedro meant when he said he was 'in the shit'.

"Pedro, I don't care how much trouble you may be in. Even if it's as bad as you say. I don't even care if your name is not Pedro—I don't care about any of that stuff. All I know is I love you."

Checking to see if his napkin was clean, Peter softly wiped the tears from Marlin's cheeks. "I'm trying hard to believe you, my darling, but I think if I tell you, the shock may kill you."

Holding the pickpocket's hand, Marlin confessed, "I'm as good as dead, anyway."

Hearing this, Peter threw caution to the wind. "Okay, I'm taking the biggest chance I've ever taken in my life."

Just as he was ready to spill the beans, Marlin's mother said, "There you are!" Not expecting to see Peter in her daughter's company, she said, "Oh, how are you, Pedro? You're here very early."

"Yes, Mrs. Mullen," Peter replied, not missing a beat, "I wanted to see Marlin exercise her horse. She really showed me some interesting moves."

Marlin pinched Peter's leg under the table. "Yes, Mum, Pedro is a fast learner—I think he'll soon be ready for the Olympics. Or if not the Olympics, then perhaps a bullring."

Mrs. Mullen didn't understand what Marlin was talking about and offered a slightly patronizing laugh. "Although I'm glad to be home, I always hate unpacking, so if you could please excuse me, I'd better go and get it done."

18

TRANSPARENCY IS only good if the one looking sees the heart.

"Pedro, I have to speak with my parents. Can we meet at Diego's cafe at noon? It's at the corner next to the club where we met."

He hesitated then replied reluctantly, "All right, see you at twelve sharp. Please don't be late." After making his way back to his hotel, he checked his pocket for his room key. Having no luck, the lovesick Scotsman knocked on the door and whispered, "Dubbsy, you there? Open the door."

Hearing a shuffle on the other side, he suspected his friend was either shadow boxing or entertaining a guest from the night before.

"Okay, give me a second. I'll be right there."

Dubbsy opened the door, wrapped in a towel. "You're back early. Did it not go well?"

Looking over at Dubbsy's occupied bed, Peter said, "It went very well, and I can see it's still going well for you."

A full head of black, curly hair and a large pair of piercing hazel eyes surfaced from beneath the sheets.

"Peter, this is…" Dubbsy's memory was failing him yet again as he tried to recall his bedmate's name. "Oh, yes, this is Consuelo."

The Latin lady gave Peter an affectionate smile and then submerged under the covers.

Peter gestured to his mate to go into the bathroom and whispered, "Does your friend speak English?"

Smiling, Dubbsy said, "Not a word. We've been communicating in sign language all night and we did wonderfully well, especially in the dark."

Peter was in no mood for his partner's casual approach. "Can you get rid of her?"

"Are you kidding me? She's a gem—I'd rather cut my throat."

Losing patience, Peter replied, "Do both of us a favor and ask her to go downstairs and get a coffee. Tell her you can meet up with her after we talk."

Dubbsy wasn't happy with the arrangement but could see from Peter's expression that something big was going down.

After Consuelo's departure, he turned to his friend. "This better be good."

Excitedly, Peter said, "She's going to London this afternoon!"

"Wait a minute. Who is she and why is she going to London?"

"You know—Marlin, the one I met at the club and robbed of her purse. Don't you remember? I read the letter to you about some clown who was going to kill himself and her. Well, since then I've…"

He hesitated.

"Yes, since then, you've what?"

Gathering his courage, he spat it out. "I've fallen in love with her."

Dubbsy started laughing. "And, yes, I've fallen in love with the girl I just asked to leave the room and have herself a coffee. Come on, pal, she's just another girl. You're a handsome bastard—you'll meet a million of them."

"Dubbs, I get that. But the thought of that stupid bastard in London topping himself and killing her would destroy me."

"Okay, pal," Dubbsy said sympathetically, "I guess we're in this together. What do you want me to do?"

Getting emotional, Peter answered, "Dubbsy, that's the thing, there isn't anything you can do, but I would ask that no matter what comes of all this, you trust me. Deal?"

Dubbsy hugged his partner, affirming they had a deal. "Peter, I'm your best pal in the world, but Consuela has been sitting downstairs for the better part of an hour. I'm going to see if she's still there. You do what you have to do, and I'll catch up with you later."

Peter sat on the bed and reread the letter addressed to the one girl he truly loved—now he feared some idiot in London was going to kill her. Checking the time, he knew he had only fifteen minutes to devise a plan. The question being, would he come clean and confess who the real Pedro Martinez was, or would he continue the masquerade?

Approaching Diego's cafe and seeing Marlin sitting there, the Glaswegian's heart began to race. "Hi, my darling, sorry if I'm four seconds late."

Marlin smiled and then began sobbing. "Pedro, my head is in a spin. I have so many problems and I want to share them with you, but I don't know where to start."

Peter took the lead. "This is what we're going to do. We're going to be totally transparent with each other. My darling, as I was saying earlier, I, too, have stuff I want to share with you, and I, also, don't know where to start. I know this is going to take a lot of trust, but if we really love each other as we say, then we'll get over it."

Marlin sat in awe of Pedro's maturity. "Okay, I agree with you, but who'll go first?"

"I feel so good about our relationship that I'm going to give you the choice, but there are two conditions. If I go first, promise me you won't run away and leave me to pay for the coffee, and secondly, we must not interrupt."

Marlin sighed, her tears of fear turning to laughter. "Okay, my matador, you're up first."

Peter took her hand and said, "Oh, shit, I was hoping you'd go first.

"Well, here we go. Remember, you said that you loved me and promised that you wouldn't change your mind no matter what?"

The lady doing the listening nodded. "I promise."

Peter took a deep breath. "Well, for a start, it's not Pedro. My name is Peter Cooney and I'm a professional pickpocket."

He expected Marlin to be shocked but was surprised to see her smiling and clapping her hands. "I love it! Tell me more."

Amazed, Peter continued with his mini-biography and noticed different facial expressions being projected from the other side of the table. When he expected a look of shock, he got a warm smile, and when he was hoping for a look of approval, instead arrows of disdain came his way. However, what really surprised the pickpocket most was that there wasn't one interruption until it came to the part when he confessed to stealing her purse.

Covering her face, Marlin began to cry. "My God, so you know."

Peter defensively said, "Know what?"

Raising her voice enough to attract the attention of those sitting nearby, she said, "Don't give me your innocent little boy shit—you knew all along. What's the matter, Pedro or Peter or whoever the hell you are? Stop feeling sorry for me."

Sensing the conversation was supplying entertainment for the other café-goers, Peter said, "Let's move from here or this conversation is over."

For a brief second, he found himself in a corridor of uncertainty. Had Marlin heard enough? Was she going break her side of the deal and not spill the promised beans?

Leaving enough peseta notes to cover three days'-worth of coffee and a generous tip for Diego's service, he walked towards the wall that separated the white sand of the Mediterranean beach and the promenade.

Marlin was caught off guard. She hadn't expected the man she dearly wanted to be her hero to walk away from the table. Her next move solidified Peter's wishes as she followed and sat beside him.

"Peter, why didn't you tell me you'd read the note?"

Calling him Peter for the first time, Marlin was sending him a signal that things were moving in the right direction.

"Listen, young lady, I'm not sure if you're in the habit of getting everything your own way, but if you truly want our relationship to go any further you'd better listen to what I have to say. After all, the agreement was to not interrupt whoever was speaking." Peter sarcastically added, "Well, I think that's what we said."

Still showing signs of tearing, Marlin said, "Okay, carry on. I won't butt in."

"If I didn't care for you even after I read that crazy bastard's note, I wouldn't have come back to your house to see you. If you remember correctly, I made no effort to get you into the sack. Surely that tells you something."

Marlin was just about to say something when he raised his hand. "Now, let's stick to the deal and I promise I won't butt in when you're speaking. The reason I came back to see you was to figure out how I could help you in the terrible situation you're in. However, since that time, I now find myself head over heels in love with you. So, whether you like it or not, I'm going to make sure this idiot doesn't get anywhere near you. I understand that you may have heard enough of my chat, but I've just one more thing to say." Taking a deep breath, he said, "Marlin Mullen, I love you with all my heart. I want you to know that someday I'm going to marry you. Now, I'm finished—you can talk for the rest of the day."

Expecting Marlin to pick up where he left off, the pickpocket was surprised and only heard the incoming tide making its way toward the little wall they were sitting on.

"Oh, please don't go all quiet on me. I'm looking forward to hearing what you have to tell me. I promise to not interrupt you."

Marlin gazed downward as if she was counting every grain of sand that lay before her.

Prompted to break the silence, Peter said, "Come on, a deal's a deal. I practically told you everything about me since the day I was born."

"Pedro…sorry, Peter…"

"Pedro is fine for the time being."

"You promised you'd not interrupt."

Peter apologized. "I'm sorry. I won't."

Wiping her eyes, she said, "My God, I thought I'd have so much to say. Now I'm struggling to put a sentence together."

True to his word, Peter sat there silently, waiting to see what might come next."

19

DON'T HESITATE *to react to a problem that has a negative impact.*

With one half of the act having just spilled his guts, the silence from the other was bordering on unbearable. Then, out of the blue, torrents of verbiage began to flow, the majority of which was found to be boring by the man who'd lived such an eventful life. Hearing about all the 'stuff' Marlin was given as a child, her horses' fancy saddles, and then her first car—none of it interested him.

As it poured forth, his mind began to wander, while under his breath he said, "I've spent the last couple of days with you and have a good picture of the abundance that has come your way. I get it. You've had a silver spoon packed in your proverbial saddlebag. Can you please move on?"

That's when it happened. "Peter, are you listening? You look bored."

Telling a lie that was far from white, he replied, "No, darling, I'm listening to every word. I'm very interested in all you're telling me."

Taking a deep breath, the lady at the podium said, "After I graduated from Oxford, that's when I met Richard."

The name Richard caught Peter's attention and he remembered the note from her purse. It had been signed "R".

Apologizing for cutting her off, he asked, "Who's Richard?"

"He's the man who sent the note you read. You know, the one you stole from my purse?" she replied with more than a hint of sarcasm.

Defensively, Peter said, "I've already apologized for that—can we move on?"

"Yes, we can move on, but I'm still hurt."

Taking an aggressive stance, Peter replied, "Listen, young lady, I'm still hurt that I was given away as a child and had to endure all the other shit, but there are things in life we can't do anything about. We've got to accept them and move on. Now, if you're going to keep reminding me of my faults and anything else I may have done that upsets you, we might as well be stopping right now. I'm not going to sit here and be lectured to."

Hearing the passion in Peter's voice, Marlin knew she'd found a man that wasn't going to be dictated to or scolded like a five-year-old. Retracting her words, she said, "I'm sorry, I didn't mean to say that. Now, let me tell you about Richard."

Peter quietly said, "Apology accepted. Go on—tell me about this bastard Richard."

Taking a deep breath, Marlin said, "He oversaw the stables and was responsible for the horses being exercised, groomed, fed and watered—you know, all the usual stuff. Plus, he helped organize transportation whenever I was competing. Initially, it was a very professional relationship, then one thing led to another and before I knew it he said he loved me and wanted to marry me."

Anxious to know how Marlin felt about the man who'd threatened to kill her, he asked, "Did you love him?"

"Absolutely not, I haven't even kissed the guy," she replied abruptly. "Please, stop interrupting me. Remember the deal—no butting in. Anyway, this guy has been hounding me for about a year and that's why I'm here in Spain. I had to get away from him. Since I've been here, he's called me at least five times a day threatening to kill himself. Then I got the note. Well, you've read it—I don't have tell you about that."

Peter took hold of the woman who had just bared her soul. "Marlin, I'm not going to ask you to trust me since I already know you do. But I am going to ask you to stay here while I go to London and see this Richard character. I promise you, no harm will come to him but, more importantly, no harm will come to me."

Holding Peter tighter, she said, "But I've promised Richard I'd go there and speak with him."

Losing his temper, Peter said, "Are you nuts? Do you want to go to London for that crazy bastard to kill you? No, this is what's going to happen. I'm going to give you the letter he sent you. Hold onto it and put it in a safe place." Scoffing, he said, "Don't let any of those nasty pickpockets get it."

Marlin was more concerned for Peter's safety than her own. "But what if he tries to hurt you? He's a really big guy."

Hoping to put his beautiful blonde at ease, he said, "I've come across big guys before and our friend Richard doesn't worry me. But what really concerns me is that you'll never go back to London without me."

Marlin couldn't put her finger on it, but instinctively knew Peter had something else on his mind. Reluctantly, she gave in and gave Peter the whereabouts of the guy who'd threatened to kill her.

"By the way, darling, before I go I have something to tell you."

Marlin expected to hear her knight in shining armor tell her how much he loved her and was surprised to hear him say, "I've never flown before and, I don't mind telling you, I'm shit-scared thinking about it."

"Don't be silly, my matador, you'll be just fine."

***

Before leaving, he told his trusted friend Dubbsy what he was planning to do. His pal, who was fast falling in love with Consuelo, was confident Peter could handle the situation.

"Peter, I know you'll take care of business, but should you hit any snags, give me a call and I'll be right over to help sort the bastard out."

Dubbsy shared the same fear of flying and said, "And just for you, I'll take a flight."

As the plane touched down in Heathrow Airport, Peter breathed a sigh of relief, happy to have his feet back on the ground. Old habits die hard, and this certainly applied to the masterful thief as he took the opportunity to pick the pockets of a few unsuspecting individuals as he quickly made his way through the international arrivals terminal.

Removing the cash and dumping the wallets, he was ready to hit the town. With his quick earnings, he now had enough money to put his head down in one of London's finest hotels.

Not only did he have the address of the man he'd journeyed to see, he also had a phone number. After enjoying a breakfast that would've choked a horse, he called to get in touch with him. Knowing his call could be traced, he opted to use a public pay phone.

Mimicking a very posh London accent, he pretended he was in the market to purchase a horse. During the course of the call, Peter explained he required his expertise, agreeing to pay for his time and any other expenses that may be incurred. He arranged to meet the equestrian expert in the city where he and Dubbsy had carried out a few transactions.

The Shamrock Inn was a typical London pub where a lot of wheeling and dealing went on. Having Richard's description, Peter recognized him immediately as he entered the upscale bar.

Approaching the six-foot-tall Richard, Peter introduced himself as Willie Campbell, asking Richard to have a seat and offering him a pint of the house special.

Obviously anxious to discuss the business of horse purchasing, Richard said, "Okay, I'll have just the one."

Putting the two pints on the table, Peter said, "You know, I've been looking forward to meeting you and, I would add, I have five friends standing outside this bar that are of the same mindset."

Wearing a puzzled expression, the horse expert hadn't a clue what was going on.

"Mr. Richard, or whatever your name is, I want you to listen to what I have to say. And let me add, it's not in your interest to leave before I'm finished—my friends outside won't be as nice as me. Now, I believe you've been calling a very dear friend of mine every hour on the hour and sending her threatening letters. I'm here to tell you, she doesn't need a fuckin' pen pal, and she doesn't appreciate you corresponding with her. And here's where I come in—if you continue to harass her, you'll not have to worry about killing yourself, it will be done for you."

The blood drained from Richard's face. "I've no idea what you're talking about, mister. You've got the wrong man."

Peter sarcastically said, "Oh, then please accept my apologies." Grabbing the guy by the back of his neck, he growled, "Listen, arse-hole, don't fuck with me. The clock behind the bar says it's two fifteen. If I spill my pint, that will be a signal to one of my associates to kill you and you'll be dead before two thirty."

Looking down, Peter could see his bluff was working big time as Richard had urinated down the leg of his trousers.

"And before you go running to the cops, I want to give you fair warning. I feel you should know a couple things about me. I'm a fair man and I believe everybody deserves a second chance. Also know, I've spent most of my life in prison and going back is no big deal. If I do go back inside, it will be worth it knowing you were taken care of by my friends."

In a state of panic, Richard said, "Okay, I'm sorry for what I did. Tell Marlin she'll never hear from me again."

"Oh, Richard, I know that, but the problem is I now have to convince my friends that you're sincere. How would you suggest I tell them you really mean what you're saying?"

The terrorized man's tears dripped into his pint glass as he mumbled, "I don't know, I don't know."

Peter continued to bluff. "Richard, this is what I'm going to do—and please, consider it a big favor. I'm going to walk outside and tell my guys that you and I have come to an understanding and everything is cool. However, if you don't keep your word, you're dead. I would suggest you don't leave this bar for at least another hour and remember everything I've said."

Leaving the bar, Peter hailed a hackney cab and returned to his five-star City Center hotel. He relaxed, had a shower, and then went down to the restaurant that only catered to the city's elite.

After being shown to his seat, he looked around and said to himself, "Dubbsy would really love this place."

After enjoying a beautifully prepared T-bone steak and all the trimmings, he finished what was left of his expensive bottle of Chardonnay. Thanking his waiter for the excellent meal and service, he returned to his room to make the international call to Marlin.

After only one ring, she answered. "Oh, Peter, I've been so worried. Are you okay, my love?"

Peter informed his sweetheart that everything had been taken care of and she had nothing more to worry about.

Dubbsy was next on the list to receive a call from London, but the pickpocket was surprised to get no response. He called many times throughout the evening and became increasingly concerned. Finally, he secured a reservation for a return flight the following morning.

20

IT'S OKAY to have your head in the clouds as long as your feet are on the ground.

Turbulence was a word the inexperienced traveler had no knowledge of, until it was announced by the British Airways flight attendant at forty thousand feet. Peter didn't even enjoy rides at the local fairground much less being tossed around in a jet-propelled tin can at such an altitude.

Relieved to have survived the ordeal, it was time to catch up with the two people that meant the most to him. Returning to base camp, he was informed by the friendly Spanish hotelier that his friend had checked out the previous day.

Where could he be?

Remembering that he and Dubbsy had met a Scottish girl who was fluent in Spanish and was a teller at a nearby bank, he made his way to enquire if she had any knowledge of his pal's whereabouts.

He also looked around to see if he could find the woman Dubbsy had fallen for, but she, too, was nowhere to be seen. Again, the anxious question began to bounce around.

Dubbsy, where are you?

Feeling a tap on his shoulder, he turned to see Dubbsy with a broad bandage wrapped around his forehead and two very bruised eyes.

"For God's sake, man, what happened to you? I've been looking all over."

"Let's get off the street—I've got a lot to tell you."

"Dubbsy, where are we going? Where's your luggage and all your stuff?"

"I'll tell you, but we have to find a place first."

Flagging a taxi, Dubbsy instructed the driver to take them to Hotel Manola.

Happy to be off the street, Dubbsy said, "Peter, when you left for London, I was sitting in the room when two guys—I mean two fuckin' bears—knocked on the door. When I opened it, they gave me a real going over... Well, you can see what they did."

"Why, Dubbsy? Why'd they do it?"

"I'll tell you why. One of the guys I dipped in the club was some Russian boxing champion and he was told it was I who stole his wallet. Well, the bastard came to the hotel to retrieve it, and retrieve he did! With a bit of interest. He and his heavyweight friend took everything I had, including our reserve fund. I'm sorry, pal. I feel I've let you down."

Gathering his thoughts, Peter said, "Listen, Dubbsy, let this be a lesson to us—from now on, we take and go."

Just as Peter was expounding on the new plan, images of Marlin's face came to his mind.

Seeing his pal deep in thought, Dubbsy said, "What's wrong? What's on your mind?"

Just as he was about answer, the taxi stopped outside a very quaint Spanish boarding house. "Okay, amigos, Hotel Manola," said the taxi driver in perfect English.

"Peter, will you pay the guy? I haven't a penny."

"No problem, Dubbsy. You're looking at a man of great wealth."

Safe and secure in their dingy room on the third floor of Hotel Manola, they sat on their smaller-than-usual single beds and traded the happenings of the past couple of days. Putting his friend at ease Peter said, "Dubbsy, don't worry, we've been in deeper shit than this."

"But, Peter, it wasn't as painful."

Taking another look at his pal's injuries, Peter said, "Dubbs, I don't care if the Russian bastards are two world champions, I'm going to even the score."

Rubbing his sore jaw, Dubbsy said, "Let's forget about it and get out of this place."

"Sure, Dubbsy, we'll leave soon, but first I've got to see Marlin."

It took him a second to remember who Marlin was, then Dubbsy said, "Peter, that reminds me. I've got to see Consuela tonight."

"You're going nowhere tonight! Please, lay low just for one night. Call her and say you'll see her tomorrow."

Peter then began counting the takings from his profitable two days in London.

Dubbsy watched as his pal stacked it into neat bundles on the bed. "For God's sake, Peter, did you rob a bank?"

"No, Dubbsy-boy, your pal Peter the Pickpocket just came across a wee bit of good fortune in Heathrow Airport, both arriving and departing. So, don't worry about money, we have plenty for the time being."

"You always seem to carry a bit of luck—I hope it never runs out."

Smiling, Peter said, "Luck is like water—you don't miss it till you need it. But for now, we have plenty of both. Now, if you'll excuse me for a couple of hours, I have to see Marlin and tell her all about that stupid bastard that was annoying her."

Peter's luck seemed to be holding. Just as he walked out of the hotel, a taxi stopped. Changing his plans at the last minute, he asked the driver to take him to a bar next to the club where Dubbsy had dipped the two Russians.

His friend's description of the two guys was very accurate and he was correct when he said they resembled bears. Peter saw them from across the room and sized them up. It was more than obvious that they were capable of clearing the bar at will.

However, the gutsy Glaswegian showed no fear, asking the gigantic bookends if they would like to do to him what they had done to Dubbsy.

The boxers laughed at the five-foot-ten, bean-pole Scotsman. "Go away, little guy, or you'll find yourself in orbit."

The aggressive Scot said, "Why don't you both step outside and we'll see who's going into orbit?"

The Russians finished off what looked like a pint of vodka and followed the bold Peter outside onto the deserted beach.

Reaching into his pocket, Peter pulled his blackwater pistol. "Right, arse-holes, get on your knees. Tonight, you're going to die."

The two immediately began to plead for clemency.

Peter slowly walked towards them. Squeezing the toy's trigger, he squirted acid into their eyes, blinding them.

"Now if you bastards come after me or my friend, it'll be worse, but something tells me you'll never find us. We'll spot your white canes a mile away."

Before leaving his victims, the merciless pickpocket squeezed the remainder of the acid directly into their faces, then beat their heads with a rock.

Walking back into the bar, he asked the Irish barman, "Paddy, did you see where those two Russians went? They said they'd come back and meet me."

The Irishman sensed something was going down. He smiled and said, "I don't know who you are, I've never seen you before, and besides, those two bastards had it coming. Now, good luck to you, but don't come back, mate."

Peter smiled, shook the barman's hand, and thanked him.

***

As the taxi pulled up at the courtyard of Granja Paloma Blanca, the coolest guy on the planet was met by Marlin's father. "Well, good evening, young man. You're just in time for dinner. I know it's late, but we have a habit of eating around nine-thirty or ten most nights. Marlin is up in her room talking to her mother—these women, once they get started there's no stopping them."

"Mr. Mullen, that's extremely kind of you, but perhaps we should run it by the ladies first."

It was obvious that Mr. Mullen had had one or two aperitifs and his Dutch courage displayed a chauvinist approach. "No, son, we don't run anything past women. We are leaders, and if they have any sense, they'll follow us."

Just then, the ladies came out of the shadow into the gas-lamp-lit courtyard. "There you are, Peter. I thought you'd never get here!"

Both parents turned with a puzzled expression. "Who's Peter? We thought it was Pedro."

As cool as ever, Peter smiled and said, "Well, it is Pedro, but strange as it may be, my middle name is Peter and Marlin prefers it."

Turning and smiling at Marlin's father, he winked and said, "Mr. Mullen, just as you were saying five minutes ago, whatever the ladies like, we must give them—a happy woman makes a happy house."

Caught off guard, Marlin's father said, "You know, son, you're a very wise young man. I agree with you one hundred percent. Now, let's go eat."

141

As they made their way to the upper patio area, Mr. Mullen whispered to the pickpocket, "You're quite a lad. You and I will get on just fine."

"Are you hungry, Peter?" inquired Marlin's mother.

"Oh, yes, Mrs. Mullen, I've not eaten since I returned from London."

"London? Why on earth did you not tell me? I would've had George fly you over," said Mr. Mullen.

Peter knew he'd dropped a clanger by mentioning London and quickly tried to cover his mistake. "Who's George?"

"George is the pilot that flies the family's private jet. The man was a fighter pilot in the Second World War."

In typical lady's fashion, Marlin's mother said, "I hope I'm not being nosy, Peter, but can I ask why you went to London for such a short time?"

Marlin looked at Peter anxiously, waiting to see how the pickpocket was going to react.

Taking a sip of wine, he said, "I'm almost embarrassed to say, but since I'm now feeling very much at home in your company, I'll tell you. Ten years ago, I underwent a surgical procedure to save my eyesight. You see, I was born with a malfunction behind my eyes and, left untreated, to put it mildly, I would have been blind. Now, every year since, I've had regular check-ups to make sure everything is in good working order."

He was so convincing, he almost had Marlin believing that was the reason for his sudden departure to the capital.

"Oh, my," said Mrs. Mullen sympathetically.

Mr. Mullen had had at least a full bottle of fine vintage on top of a few aperitifs and said from the other end of the table, "I didn't catch all of that. Did you say you went to London to buy blinds?"

Irritated with her father, Marlin replied, "No, Dad, he wasn't buying blinds. I'll tell you in the morning."

Peter gave his Wonder Woman a smile, and signaled it was time to leave her parents to finish what remained of the evening. Excusing himself, he said, "Mr. and Mrs. Mullen, thank you for such a delightful evening. I really enjoyed the wonderful meal, but more importantly, I enjoyed your company. Now, if you don't mind, I'd like to tell Marlin all about my experience in London."

As Peter and their daughter left the table, Marlin's parents looked at each other. Without saying a word, they hoped Peter was the one for their precious Marlin.

21

IN GLASS HOUSES, don't throw stones—sponges may be the wiser choice.

A while later, an embarrassed Mrs. Mullen asked Peter for some assistance. She needed help getting the man of the house back to his room—he was showing the effects of having consumed one too many glasses of the fine wine.

Later, Mr. Mullen was safe in bed although fully clothed. His grateful wife thanked Peter for his help.

Returning to Marlin, the young lovers made their way across the dimly lit courtyard.

"Peter, I'm so embarrassed. My Dad doesn't know when he's had enough—I think he would drink till he fell flat on his face."

Peter defended the man he hardly knew. "Don't be silly, we're all human. That's just your dad's way of escaping from his reality, whatever that may be."

His philosophical reply caused Marlin to weep. "My darling, you're so right. He's in so much shit, it's driving my poor mum and me crazy."

"If you don't mind me asking, what kind of shit are we talking about?"

Marlin hesitated. "I wasn't going to tell you, but what the hell, I think we are well past keeping secrets. The reason my Dad is here in Spain is because he's wanted in the UK in connection with some major fraud against four of Britain's major lending institutions. Don't ask me what he did—I've no clue, but I can't stand the thought of him going to prison for the rest of his life."

After opening up about her Dad's troubles, Marlin exclaimed, "My God, what a mess we're all in."

Peter tried to inject a bit of humor into the situation. "Don't worry. I know a guy who robs people every day in the week, and yet he walks down the street as if he's doing the community a service."

"Who would that be?" asked the inquisitive Marlin.

"Tony Callaghan, the bookie," Peter said. "I think there are many people who appear to be as honest as the day is long— you know, upright citizens of this world—yet they'd steal the eyes out of your head. Then there are those who get the reputation for being crooks, and they're probably the most honest of the bunch."

Marlin sat on the foot of her bed, mesmerized with Peter's take on life.

"I've only known your father a short while, but I can tell he's no crook. The reason I say this is I've lived my whole life surrounded by them."

Seeing his date getting sleepy, the pickpocket checked his watch and suggested he go back to his hotel.

"Oh, no, darling, please stay with me tonight. I would really like you to stay." The girl who was used to getting it all her own way protested.

Peter held her and said, "I'm not going far—we're talking a taxi ride away. I've got to see Dubbsy—he's feeling a bit under the weather. I promise I'll come see you tomorrow."

Hotel Manola was a far cry from the luxurious hotel he'd had in England's capital, yet knowing Dubbsy was out of harm's way gave him a sense of comfort that no five-star accommodation could provide.

"I thought you'd never be back," Dubbsy said as his pal entered the room. "I've been lying here worried, thinking those two Russians would be back to give me another hiding."

Clearing his throat, the pickpocket said, "The two bears who roughed you up will never see you again."

The injured man lying on the other bed said, "What makes you so sure? Sometimes guys like to beat you up just for the sake of it."

Sounding quite confident, Peter assured his pal no more harm would come to him by the Russians.

Not convinced, Dubbsy asked again, "But what makes you so sure?"

Wanting to put his pal's mind at rest once and for all, Peter replied, "You know me, Dubbsy, and when I say the problem is solved, believe me, it's solved. Don't ask me how—just know that I made it go away."

Looking to the bed opposite and seeing his pal in a deep sleep eliminated any feelings of guilt regarding the payback he'd administered to the two boxers. Then drifting into a deep sleep himself, he dreamt that Marlin's father was found guilty by the highest court in the land. As he was being led away, Peter heard Marlin cry out, "Dad! Dad! Don't worry, Peter will get you off!"

Dubbsy heard Peter moaning and talking in his sleep. Shaking his shoulder, he said, "Peter, Peter, are you okay? I think you were having a bad dream."

Looking physically shaken, Peter jumped up. "What time is it?"

Trying to put his friend at ease, Dubbsy said, "It's still early. It's only eight thirty."

Rubbing his eyes, the pickpocket said, "I was dreaming that I was a lawyer defending Marlin's dad."

Dubbsy laughed. "Please don't tell me he's also a pickpocket."

"No, the guy's so stinking rich, it would blow your mind."

Dubbsy excitedly said, "Good for you, pal. Don't marry for love, marry for money—it seems to work out better."

"Believe it or not, Dubbs, as much as I think I love the richest woman on the planet, I really don't want to marry her. There is just something about her I'm not sure of. I just can't put my finger on it."

Looking into his pal's eyes, Dubbsy said, "Peter, my good man, try to like her and I promise to be your faithful gardener for the rest of my life."

Peter ran his hands through his hair. "Dubbsy, what in God's name are we doing with our lives? Here we are, stuck in the middle of Spain like two redundant bullfighters. We can't be picking pockets for the rest of our days."

Peter's reality check took Dubbsy by surprise as he was of the opinion they would just drift through life until the story ended. Now his best friend was talking about bursting the bubble yet offering no alternative.

***

No longer a stranger and being guaranteed the proverbial welcome on the mat, Peter returned to the estate that was beginning to feel like home.

"Hello, young Peter," said the man whom he'd helped carry to bed the night before.

"Hello, Mr. Mullen, how are you feeling this morning?"

"Absolutely wonderful!"

It was obvious the man had no recollection of his legless state a mere fifteen hours earlier and showed no ill effects from the beverages he had consumed. Then, before Peter could ask the whereabouts of Marlin, the energetic Mr. Mullen said, "Peter, I need a word with you."

Conscious of the necessity of staying on the right side of the wealthy man, Peter confidently replied, "Sure, Mr. Mullen, what's on your mind?"

Ushering the young con-man to a quiet corner near the stables, he said, "Peter, you and I have something in common."

Not wanting to second guess the man who had initiated the conversation, he remained silent, hoping the old gentleman would get straight to the point.

"I have a feeling you are not who you say you are. What makes me say such a thing is, I've lived the same lie all my life."

Taking the bull by the horns, Peter said, "Mr. Mullen, you may not be Mr. Mullen, but in me, what you see is what you get. Now with respect, I ask that you get to the point. What exactly are you asking me? Or is this some sort of game you want to play? I don't play games, so if there's something you want to know, I promise I'll tell you. It may not be what you want hear, but nevertheless, you'll have an answer."

Not expecting Peter's bold approach, the property tycoon found himself speechless.

"Let me put you straight, Sir. Firstly, you're talking to the man who helped carry you to bed last night. Secondly, if you're of the impression I'm hanging around here to get whatever I can from your daughter, you're sadly mistaken. The only reason I'm here is because I love Marlin, not for what money you have or, perhaps, don't have."

The man of the house interrupted. "What are you getting at, young man?"

"No, Mr. Mullen, What are *you* getting at? You brought me over here to tell me something, so say whatever you have to say.

Then I'll be on my way and leave you to count your money before it quickly disappears."

The old man was really struggling with Peter's attitude. "Okay, I'll tell you why I wanted to talk with you. When we first met, you gave me some bullshit that your name was Pedro something or other. Now, you're Peter Cooney. You said you just graduated from Strathclyde—another lie."

Peter was ready to interrupt but Mullen held his ground. "I didn't stop you talking, so now do the proper thing and let me finish. Where was I? Yes, you give me a whole load of crap about your eyesight. Come on, son, let's get things straight. Believe me, I'll think more of you if you're honest with me. So, tell me who you are. I want to be open with you."

The pickpocket found himself on the defensive and had visions of giving the father the same confession he'd given to his daughter.

"Mr. Mullen, what I have to say will take a bit of time. Can I ask that we meet later, and I'll tell you all? But there's one condition."

"What's the condition?"

Peter said, "I want you to be as transparent with me as I'll be with you."

Shaking hands, the deal was made.

"Now, if you don't mind, sir, I'd like to go and see your pretty daughter."

***

"What were you and Dad talking about? It sounded as if you were ready to fight."

Peter smiled. "There would be no chance of that—the guy would kill me!"

22

A DIFFERENCE of opinion doesn't have to suggest one is right and one is wrong.

Marlin's obsession for horses and Peter's indifference towards the beasts was having a detrimental effect on the relationship.

In as much as Peter wished only to be in the company of his blonde bombshell, the smell of horse manure and the flies it attracted, were beginning to repel the city slicker.

"Marlin, let's meet in town for lunch—the fresh sea air will be a change from the odors that are coming from that horse shit."

Although annoyed with what was being said, Marlin semi-pleaded with her lover. "Oh, Peter, I really hope you'll get used to equestrian life. I find it so invigorating to be with the horses."

The quick-witted Scot's response didn't amuse the woman of the saddle. "I find it quite invigorating to be around you, but I detest being up to my knees in horse shit."

The obvious breakdown in communication led Peter to take a firm stance. "I'm going back to the hotel to check on Dubbsy. When you've had your fill of horses for one day and are hungry, I'll meet you at our usual place. I'll be there at two. If Dubbsy is feeling better, I hope you don't mind but I'd like to invite him, also."

Arriving at the hotel, Peter couldn't understand what all the commotion was. The police had the hotel surrounded.

"Señor, your friend is dead!"

Looking around, Peter thought it was Alberto Manola, the hotelier, speaking to someone else in the crowd until he put his arm on his shoulder and repeated, "Señor Peter, two men came to my hotel this morning asking for you. Then I heard *Bang! Bang!* I go to your room and your friend is dead on the floor. I am so sorry, Señor."

The pickpocket was in a state of shock. He couldn't accept what he was being told. Dropping to his knees, he screamed, "I'll get the bastards!"

"Excuse me, sir," a police officer said in perfect English, "is your name Peter Cooney?"

Still dazed, he replied very quietly, "Yes, yes, I'm Peter Cooney, but how do you know my name?"

The officer pulled a passport from his breast pocket. "My men found your passport and other personal effects belonging to you and your deceased friend under his mattress."

Oblivious to the police captain's findings, Peter said, "Can I see Dubbsy? Are you sure he's dead?"

In a matter of fact tone, the officer replied, "Oh, yes, Mr. Dubbsy is quite dead, and we need you to identify the body."

With all the commotion, Peter was having difficulty taking in what was being said. Then, looking across the road, he recognized the two victims of the acid-filled water pistol attack.

As they hid in the shadow of a shop doorway, they smiled through their heavily banged faces, drawing their hands across their throats indicating he was next.

The pickpocket screamed, "You bastards are going to die!"

Two policemen restrained the heartbroken Scot, and the captain said, "Mr. Cooney, please come with us. I have some questions for you."

As he sat alone, sobbing and staring at the whitewashed walls of the dimly lit interrogation room, the only thing to break the monotony was a picture of the king and queen of Spain hanging from the backdrop of flaking paint.

Two o'clock had come and gone, and lunch with Marlin was the furthest thing from his saddened mind. The pickpocket's memories replayed over and over. "Why did I not finish those two bastards off when I had the chance? Dubbsy would still be with me."

The guilt-ridden Scot was quickly reaching the point of no return. Revenge was all that occupied his mind, and how he was going to even the score on the two that had killed Dubbsy.

The light bulb that hung over the old, dark green painted table could not have been any more than thirty watts. It swayed back and forth due to the draft created when the police captain opened the door to enter the room.

"Señor Cooney, can I get you some coffee or perhaps tea? I know you English like to drink tea."

"I'm Scottish, not English," retorted Peter, establishing his heritage, then politely declining the captain's offer.

"Now, Señor Cooney, let's go back to the night you and your friend did the robbery."

Protesting, Peter replied, "Robbery? What are you talking about?"

"Mr. Cooney, I'm not here to waste time. You either cooperate with me or I'll make it difficult for you. Señor, when I say difficult, I mean *very* difficult. Do we understand each other? The choice is yours."

Being addressed as Mr. Cooney, then moments later hearing Señor Cooney was frustrating the man on the hot seat. Not knowing the extent of the evidence, the interrogating officer had on him, the perplexed pickpocket said, "Okay, captain, what would you like to know?"

Inhaling the smoke from his half-smoked cigar, the captain blew a perfect ring. "As you say in your country, 'A very wise move.' By cooperating with me, this means we all get to go home soon. I am sure you don't want to be sitting here into the night."

Taking the 'good cop' approach, the captain said, "Now, my friend, tell me all about yourself."

Hearing the captain putting emphasis on the word ALL caused Peter to think about the questions Marlin's father had for him. That coupled with his preoccupation as to how accurately the captain could blow rings of cigar smoke that haloed the solitary light bulb put his mind elsewhere. His wandering was interrupted when the captain raised his voice. "Señor Cooney, I'll ask you again to tell me about yourself."

The captain's tone indicated it would be in his best interest to comply.

"Well, my name is Peter Cooney. I was born and raised in the west of Scotland."

The man being questioned began to muse over the term 'raised'. Smiling, he figured the nearest he ever got to being raised was on his maiden flight to London.

Continuing, Peter went into all the crappy details from his infancy to being informed his best friend in the world had just been shot.

After compiling many notes, the captain threw his pen on the desk. "My friend, you've had a very challenging life. I think my report will be missing some details which will be to your advantage."

Sensitive to fact the captain was cutting him some slack, Peter said, "You know, I may have had some unlucky breaks in life, but I'm also very grateful for those who have helped me along the way, and you're one of those people, El Capitán, mi amigo. Gracias."

The police captain smiled at the pickpocket's efforts to speak Spanish. After informing Peter there would be no further need to speak with him in connection with the sad circumstances relating to the untimely death of his friend, the captain handed him his passport and the personal belongings of his dear friend Dubbsy.

Having identified the remains, the effects of the circumstances of his death were weighing heavily on the young Scotsman's shoulders. Still having to deal with the threat of the Russians, meeting with Marlin's father was fast fading into insignificance. Wanting to inform Marlin of the tragic circumstances that had caused his absence for the lunch date, he made his way to the estate, only to be greeted with the cold shoulder.

"Peter, I waited one hour for you, for our so-called lunch date, and you failed to appear. How could you be so heartless as to not contact me?"

Rather than explain himself, the distraught pickpocket turned and walked toward the entrance gate. "Perhaps someday, you'll be fortunate enough to hear why I wasn't there. Don't come looking for me as I won't be easily found."

Marlin's father was standing in the shadows and heard the confrontation. "Just let him go, dear. He's bad news. You deserve far better than that scoundrel."

Not sure what to do next or where to go, the loneliest man in the world wandered along the unpaved road toward town. The longer he walked, the sadder he became at the loss of his best friend. No more extravagant planning. No more Italian meals in Barnardi's restaurant. No more working together doing what they did best. All these thoughts brought a sadness to him that he never thought possible.

Walking aimlessly, he found himself at an old building on a piece of farm property. Feeling really fatigued, he decided to rest for a while, knowing he'd be safe and out of harm's way from those who'd murdered Dubbsy.

After a night's sleep in the hay, he was awakened by the sound of a couple roosters on the other side of a dilapidated old shed. Walking outside, he was met by a shotgun pointed at his chest. For a second, he thought it would be better if the man holding the antique weapon would just pull the trigger. That would solve all his problems and he wouldn't have to hide from the murdering Russians. Or explain himself to some guy the British police were chasing, or deal with his spoiled daughter.

Realizing Peter's Spanish was non-existent, the old farmer gestured that he put his hands behind his head and follow him to the main house. Once inside the cozy cottage, he was told in Spanish to sit.

As he took the proffered seat, in walked the police captain who had interviewed him the previous day. "Señor Cooney, please don't tell me you tried to rob mi primo...sorry, my cousin?"

Protesting his innocence, Peter said, "I got lost on the country road and was very tired, so I thought I'd rest and fell asleep in the old building."

The police captain played the role of interpreter and explained to the old farmer and his wife the circumstances of how the pickpocket came to be on their property.

"My cousin apologizes for his aggressive behavior and asks if you'd like to have some breakfast?"

Somewhat relieved the police captain was on hand to help both his cousin and himself, Peter said, "Yes, please, I'm really hungry, but please tell your cousin I'd like to pay him for his hospitality."

The irate captain said, "Señor, I will tell my cousin no such thing. When you are a guest in this country, you don't pay anything. That would offend my cousin and his dear wife Maria."

Having enjoyed the breakfast and Spanish hospitality, Peter thanked the farmer and his wife very much and asked the police captain for directions to town.

"My friend, I would advise you not to go into town. My informants tell me that you are wanted by some individuals from the Russian community. I think it is best you stay here with my cousin for the time being."

23

THE GRASS *isn't always greener, it may just be a different shade.*

Life as a Spanish farm hand had never been a consideration to the man whose life had gravitated around the hustle and bustle of the city. After all, there were no pockets to pick in the middle of an empty field—just the odd cow that required milking.

As the days passed, the tranquil environment became more appealing, although Peter couldn't get conditioned to the various smells that went hand-in-hand with country living.

Initially, he was under the impression he would be hanging around Fernando and Maria's farm for no more than a day or so. Now that the third week was fast approaching, he began to wonder if the friendly police captain had forgotten about his newfound Scottish amigo.

"There you are, my friend, have you enjoyed life on my cousin's farm? He tells me you are becoming more proficient in the Spanish language."

The police captain then asked Peter if he would like to join him for dinner in the city—he had a plan that he wanted to share with him.

Curiosity getting the better of him, Peter asked the captain what he had in mind.

Keeping him in suspense, the captain said, I'll tell you tonight over dinner, my friend."

Now quite the expert in operating the tractor and plow, Peter drove up and down the fields for the remainder of the day trying to guess what the captain had to say. Right on the stroke of six, he heard two pumps on the punctual policeman's horn.

Greeting the captain, he said. "Buenas noches, Señor, cómo está?"

Wishing to continue the conversation in his native tongue, the policeman replied, "Bien, gracias, y usted, también?"

Now on first-name terms, Tomás asked Peter if he was enjoying the simple life of working on a Spanish farm.

Peter replied, "It is certainly different from what I'm used to."

The waiter filled the table with an assortment of local dishes, and Tomás said, "I hope you'll enjoy what I have ordered."

Peter's appetite was more focused towards the captain's plan than what lay before him. "It all looks fantastic, Tomás, however I'm more interested in what you have to tell me."

Chewing on a piece of chicken, the captain said, "Oh, yes, the plan. I have an idea that should benefit both of us."

Now enjoying the local delicacies and with his mouth half full, Peter asked Tomás what his plan was.

"We have something in common and that is, we both need to dispose of the Russians. They have come to this city of mine with drugs and prostitutes and, as the Chief of Police, it's giving me many headaches."

Continuing to listen, Peter was anxious to see where he fit into the captain's plan.

"I need to get rid of these people and here is how I propose to do it. If a non-Spanish citizen is found carrying an illegal substance, he will be deported immediately. These guys are very smart, and it is almost impossible to find drugs on them. Here is where you come in, Peter, my friend. You are very skillful at taking things out of people's pockets—what I need you to do, is put things *into* their pockets."

Peter interrupted. "Drugs."

"Exactly," replied the Spanish policeman. "I need you to bump into them, or do whatever you do, and place the drugs in their pockets. When that is done, my men and I will take it from there."

The captain looked at his guest's plate still filled with food. "You're not eating. Don't you like the food?"

Peter apologized. "Yes, Tomás, it's excellent, but I was more interested in listening to what you were saying."

The pickpocket who regarded himself as a planner, asked the man doing the planning how he intended to execute his idea. After he posed the question, it was obvious the captain had put a lot of thought and consideration into his scheme to get the bad guys off his streets.

"Okay, this is how we are going to catch the rats. My informants assure me there are nine at the center of their operation. So, we are going to take them not one at a time, but three at a time."

Peter was anxious to know where he fit in. "Sounds all fine and dandy."

Looking puzzled, the inspector asked, "What is fine and dandy? I never hear such words before."

Peter apologized again. "It means it all sounds very simple, but how are you going to arrange for three Russian gangsters to be in the same place, at the same time, so I can drop something into their pockets?"

The captain smiled. "I'm going to organize...let's call it a little fiesta just for them and their amigos, and you will also be invited."

Peter protested. "No way, captain. If I show up and I'm recognized by our comrades, I'm a dead man."

The master planner smiled. "Do you not think that I've not taken that into consideration, my friend? Besides, I need you if I'm to take this to a satisfactory conclusion."

The captain continued, "My men will have you covered twenty-four hours a day until the bastards are deported."

Although he still had his doubts, something told Peter the captain would fulfill his promise and get him back to England safe and well.

***

The party was in full swing.

The pickpocket had been advised who his victims were—all he had to do was play the reverse roll. Instead of taking, he was now giving.

Walking to the bar, he asked two rather large guys to excuse him as he was trying to order a drink. Just as they stepped aside, the skilled fingersmith made the drop.

The undercover police got the nod from Peter that the deed was done, and moved in, bringing the party to a halt.

Having a Russian interpreter on hand to avoid any miscommunication, the captain said to the three heavyset, well-tanned foreigners that they were under arrest for being in possession of narcotics which was against the law in his country.

Furiously protesting, the three not-so-wise men were shocked to see the drugs removed from their pockets.

As the culprits were led away, Peter lurked in the shadows. *Three down, six to go.*

The fiesta was over in more ways than one. After boarding the prearranged taxi, the pickpocket returned to life as a peasant farmer.

Putting the first three away was relatively easy compared to what lay ahead. The challenge that faced both the policeman with the bright ideas, and the pickpocket with the slick fingers, was that the remaining six Russians were bound to be extra vigilant, so another fiesta was out of the question.

For the capture of the next three, Peter would devise a strategy. When he informed the captain that he had a plan, the Spaniard was only too willing to hear what the pickpocket had to say.

"Tomás, these guys are not stupid. We now have to approach the situation from a different perspective."

"Sí, my friend, let's hear it."

"Forget about drugs, let's play the Russians at Russian roulette."

The captain looked puzzled. "I'm not following you."

Excited and with confidence, Peter said, "Okay, here's what we do. I know it's going to be risky, nevertheless, it's going to work. I'll go and meet the guys you're trying to get rid of and will tell them I want to buy their drugs. I'll arrange to meet them near the airport, telling them I'm taking a flight to England. I'll have a case with the money, they'll have a case with the drugs, and I'll let them escape with the money. That will give them confidence that I'm for real. We will put the word on the street that I made bail, then we'll repeat the procedure. On round two, I'll hand over a case which will be lined with drugs. After the swap, you pounce."

The captain's skepticism was causing Peter to doubt his own plan, however, after debating back and forth, he convinced the police chief it would work. The following ten days were the most hectic of Peter's life. Picking pockets was one thing, but this was uncharted territory—definitely a case of do or die.

The second stage of the plan reached a more-than-successful conclusion due to the fact that four members of the gang were captured in the ambush. In Peter's mind, it was seven down and two to go.

However, the captain knew Peter was more interested in the final two—they were the men responsible for Dubbsy's murder.

"Peter, I'd like to offer you some advice. Whether you take it or not, I've no control, but please don't put me in a very uncomfortable situation."

Peter understood what the friendly captain was trying to say. "Please leave the remaining two Russians to my men and myself. I don't want you to get involved with them as the outcome could prove to be very sad, especially for you, my friend."

The pickpocket was of the opinion he was being short-changed. After all, he'd helped put the first seven away—the last two were the icing on the cake.

"Captain, say what you like, but I'm going to take care of those animals who killed Dubbsy."

The captain knew his words fell on deaf ears, but finished by saying, "I wish you well, my friend. Please go home to your beloved Scotland. You are still a young man—you can't change the past, but you can certainly change your future."

The Spaniard gave the Scotsman a farewell hug. "Dios vaya contigo."

24

FREE ADVICE can be very costly.

Choosing to ignore the captain's words of caution, Peter's focus was undeterred. He was aware that his steps had to be covered two-fold. On one hand, two Russians were in hot pursuit; on the other, he had God knows how many policemen surveilling him.

Overwhelming as it may have been, the conundrum had to be addressed even if the revenge for Dubbsy's killing would result in his own demise. Although he had great respect for the police captain, he thought it better to ignore his advice and decided to remain on the Costa Brava. This would afford him the opportunity to strategize a course of action that would eliminate the two remaining unwanted guests of the sleepy coastal town.

The cop and robber now on friendly terms never discussed each other's passions, just as Peter wasn't aware that Dubbsy had an interest in trains till he spoke about them just before his death. And the other half of the act hadn't shared with his deceased friend that he was passionate about Scottish history.

Sitting on the hot sandy beach, again admiring the scenery, Peter began to recall some Scottish historical facts and customs, some of which, in his skeptical mind could be categorized as old tales. For example, in days gone by, before a villain was executed, he was offered a final drink of the hard stuff to see him on his way to pastures new. Whether it was true or not didn't matter, but the story gave the pickpocket an idea.

The stakes would be high—a definite case of 'winner takes all.' He would purposely make himself available to his assailants. He knew if his gamble didn't pay off, he would be joining Dubbsy.

Familiar with all the busy and not-so-busy cantinas in town, he knew where to find the people he desperately wanted to take revenge upon. Visiting the popular night spot, he made no attempt to be inconspicuous in the hope the Russian sharks would take the bait and spot him immediately.

Through their blurred vision, the man who had inflicted their serious injuries was recognized instantly, and the comrades wasted no time in forcefully inviting the daring Scot to the rear of the premises.

The pickpocket made the feeble excuse that he wanted to apologize and let by-gones be by-gones.

The two hooligans would have none of it and began to rough their victim up. The pickpocket lay bruised and bleeding but could see everything was going according to plan. In between kicks and punches, he moaned, "Okay, you're going to kill me, but there's an old Scottish tradition, and you coming from a country of many traditions will surely respect mine. Before you kill me, be sure to have one last drink with me."

The bruised Scot reached into his pocket and produced a small flask of vodka. Pretending to gulp some down, he then passed the lethal cocktail of vodka laced with an undetectable poison to the Russians.

In their greed, they each poured enough of the deadly substance down their throats to lead to instant death. Mission accomplished.

Peter quickly gathered his belongings and fled from the Spanish town without trace, leaving the two corpses that had robbed him of his best friend.

When word reached police headquarters that the remaining two Russians would no longer be causing problems, the captain smirked, ignoring his suspicions that the pickpocket was the prime suspect. It was apparent that solving the case of who killed the unwanted Soviets wasn't high on his list of priorities.

The mild-mannered captain felt it would be more convenient to view their deaths as the result of an unfortunate accident with no suspicious circumstances attached.

Secure in familiar surroundings, the Clock Bar still looked as it did the day Peter had sampled his first pint of dark ale. The only thing missing was Dubbsy. Without him being around to share in the banter, things would never be the same.

The barman, Joe Rooney, inquired of the pickpocket's friend.

Without going into the sickening details, Peter replied, "He had a bit of misfortune when we were in Spain—I suppose he's in a better place."

Seeing the hurt on the pickpocket's face at the loss of his dear friend, Joe Rooney said, "You have my sympathies, young fellow."

Thanking the barman, he then ordered many more pints. Rooney, seeing the over-consumption that was taking place by the grieving pickpocket, put a halt to the proceedings. "Young man, I realize you're missing your good mate, but swallowing pint after pint is not going to change the situation. I suggest you go home now and try to get some sleep."

No longer having the company of his confidant, the grieving Peter found himself in a world of hurt and loneliness that offered no hope. In his depressive state, he questioned if he should take a large drink of the cocktail he'd administered to the Russians.

The barman's advice came a bit too late, as he had already consumed more of the house dark ale than he could handle.

Awakening the next morning with a throbbing headache, it was then he promised himself he would never touch another drop of alcohol. After washing and shaving off a four-day growth, the fresher-faced reflection in the bathroom mirror spoke. "Okay, Peter, boy! What's it to be? Back to the Clock Bar, or make this the first day of a new beginning?"

Still feeling slightly hungover, the answer came easy. "I'm a pickpocket and I'll return to my craft for the time being."

In the months that followed, the new and improved Peter Cooney accumulated enough cash that his reserves allowed him to venture into the secondhand and antique furniture business. This new line of work could not be attributed to chance, but to divine intervention.

One busy Saturday morning as he was leaving Baker Street underground station, he was spotted plying his trade and relieving a well-dressed gentleman of his wallet. The person witnessing the pickpocket's criminal act was none other than the right Reverend Russell Pendexter.

After the dip was successfully executed, the pickpocket hurried his steps. The vigilant minister made it a point to stay in pace with the thief.

"Excuse me, sir, can I have a word?" asked the very polite collared gentleman.

Replying to the question, the cocky pickpocket said, "That would depend on the subject matter."

The minster took some deep breaths and said, "I'm not as young as I once was. If we can slow the pace down, it would be appreciated."

The pickpocket acknowledged the old man's request, thinking respect should be the order of the day. "Okay, let's stop for a minute. What can I do for you?"

The clergyman said, "Oh, it's not what you can do for me, young man, it's what I can do for you. As you can see, I'm a minister of the church, however, I'm not on a mission to convert strangers on the street. I'm here to tell you that I watched you pick a man's pocket as you left Baker Street underground station, and I'd like to compliment you on your technique."

The pickpocket was caught slightly off guard with the stranger's statement. "What is this? Some kind of joke?"

"No, it's certainly not a joke, and I suspect the person who's pocket you stole from won't see it as a joke either."

Getting straight to the point, the one in possession of the stolen wallet said, "Okay, mister, what exactly do you want?"

Out of breath, the minister replied, "Can we sit on that bench over there?"

"Sure, why not?"

The men who were strangers to each other sat in the warmth of the afternoon sun.

Peter said, "I don't know your name, although I detect a slight Scottish accent."

Apologizing, the vigilant old man offered his hand. "Pendexter, Russell Pendexter."

With a tone of pride in his voice, Pendexter said, "You certainly do detect a Scottish accent. I was born in the Fife, in the city of Saint Andrews, and spent the first eighteen years of my life there. Then we moved to India. My father was a member of the Royal Air Force, so he was stationed in quite a few countries. Before he left the service, he was stationed in the outskirts of London and that is where we finally settled."

The more the pickpocket listened to Russell Pendexter, the more interested he became.

"Is your father from Scotland?"

"No, but my mother is. Her maiden name is Russell, hence my first name. She was born just outside Glasgow in the town of Airdrie."

Having given the pickpocket his name and background, he said, "Now tell me a bit about yourself, young man."

Shaking Pendexter's hand, he said, "Peter Cooney. As far as I know, I was born in the east end of Glasgow, but God only knows who to."

Inquisitively, Pendexter said, "I'm not sure what you mean."

"Oh, it's a long story," Peter murmured. "This is a very strange situation. You've just witnessed me dipping some guy, you tell me how much you admire my technique, and then you want to know all about me. With the greatest of respect, I won't be giving you my confession anytime soon."

"Nor would I want to hear it. I believe that's between you and the Lord Himself."

A somewhat relieved Peter said, "Well, that's good because I've done so many wrong things in my life I wouldn't know where to start."

Putting his hand on the pickpocket's shoulder, Russell Pendexter said, "You may not believe it, but I could keep you here all day if I were to confess my sins to you. It is said, 'Don't judge the book by the cover.' I'm a classic example of that. I wasn't always a man of God."

Checking his watch, the minister said, "Peter, I'd love to talk to you more, but I have an appointment."

As Pendexter stood to leave, he handed Peter the wallet he had witnessed him take from the man at the station. "You're a good pickpocket, but you've a lot to learn, my friend. Here is my number—call me when you have time."

The pickpocket sat amazed as the slick-fingered man of God walked away.

25

LETTING SLEEPING DOGS lie can lead to great unrest.

"You have reached Saint Steven's Church Hempstead. Please leave a message after the tone."

When trying to contact the Reverend Russell Pendexter, Peter reached a recorded greeting that sounded like a broken record, but he continued his efforts. It was after his fourteenth attempt that he decided to leave a number where he could be contacted, should the good pastor wish to get in touch.

Instead, he focused his attention on the busy shopping season that was fast approaching, knowing it would be difficult to ply his trade without Dubbsy's aid. Having his long-time pal distracting the victim made the task much easier, nevertheless, if he was to take advantage of the vulnerable prey, the show had to go on.

Due to a strong advertising campaign on radio and television, shoppers came out in droves in search of the various items being pitched, but as word spread, people became more aware of the threat of pickpockets. This meant the fingersmith had to up his game to avoid being caught in the act—he knew fresh methods of distraction had to be deployed.

One of his best tricks was to drop some loose change in front of his target hoping to get some sympathy. While the good Samaritan was bending down to help collect the dropped coins, he would make the dip.

Safely back home, taking inventory of the day's take, the pickpocket noticed a business card with the name John McKenna, Chief Executive Officer, Texas Oil, in one of the wallets.

Having no clue what 'chief executive officer' meant, after further inspection he saw that the wallet contained various credit cards. The thief put them aside for further consideration.

Then, out of the blue, the phone rang. "Hello, Peter, it's Russell here, Pendexter."

"Hello, Russell," Peter answered, without any great enthusiasm.

"I realize you've been trying to get hold of me. I must apologize—I was attending one of those ecclesiastical conferences."

The caller's delivery didn't quite ring true and Peter had a sneaking suspicion something wasn't quite right.

"Not a problem, Russell, but let's meet up sometime soon."

Pendexter sensed he was getting the cold shoulder. "Let's make it sooner rather than later. How about lunch tomorrow? I'll meet you at the entrance to Baker Street next to Thompson's, the news agent."

The pickpocket reluctantly agreed.

Punctuality could have been Peter's middle name, as he was on time every time.

"Glad you could make it," the clergyman said warmly.

Still showing no great eagerness about his lunch date, Peter replied dryly, "Thanks for asking me."

The pastor made it obvious the venue had been prearranged. "Is Chinese good for you?"

The question indicated Peter really had no choice.

He played along. "That sounds good—it's been a while since I've had good Chinese food."

Peter was impressed by the pastor's technique with the chopsticks and said, "You're better with those chopsticks than I am with a knife and fork."

Letting the compliment go over his head, Russell said, "I've lived in many countries and spent much time in Hong Kong. I'm afraid it was a case of 'when in Rome,' but I don't like the idea of eating pizza with chopsticks."

Peter offered a patronizing smile. "Well, I'm no Roman or Chinese, so I'll just stick to using a knife and fork."

Throughout the meal, the conversation hovered around the peripheral, then Peter, bold as ever, said, "Something tells me Russell isn't really your name...and what's more, if you're a pastor, I'm the next Pope."

The man who was skillfully maneuvering his chopsticks through the mound of Chinese noodles almost choked. He swallowed and said, "You're very perceptive, and you're right on both counts. My name isn't Russell Pendexter—but you must admit it sounds good—and secondly, I'm not a man of God. In fact, I'm more of a devil."

Peter threw down his fork. "I knew it! I flipping knew it! But I must admit, you nearly had me fooled."

After shaking his dinner guest's hand, the pastor said, "By the way, here's your watch."

"How'd you do that?" Peter exclaimed, almost falling off his chair.

Once again, he shook the young fingersmith's hand and said in a strong Glaswegian accent, "Let me introduce myself—my name is James Slavin." Then, lowering his voice, he said, "Peter, I've been playing the game since long before you were born, but I must say, when I watched you operate the other day, I was impressed by your technique. It was really smooth, but like anything else, there is always room for improvement."

Peter had initially hoped he was meeting a man of God for some spiritual guidance, but he was now being mentored by a master of the pickpocket profession. Desperate to know everything about his new pick-pocketing professor, he asked, "What gave you the idea to come up with all that pastor shit?"

Looking around, James said, "If you're done eating, let's get out of here. There are far too many people and security cameras."

As they left the restaurant, it began to rain. Both men ran for shelter under a shop canopy, and James laughingly said, "I'd ask you back to the church, but unfortunately, it's closed on Thursday."

"Aye, ya bastard, I bet it's closed on Sunday, also."

James removed the pastoral collar and suggested they go for a beer.

As anxious as Peter was to learn from the master, he said, "No thanks, as much as I would really enjoy a drink, it could be the death of me."

"I've said that a thousand times," James replied thoughtfully, "but I just keep going back for more."

Having a change of heart, Peter thought, What the hell, I'll go and get a soft drink."

James had bought dinner and Peter knew it was only right that he buy the first round of drinks. The waiter delivered a double whiskey and a half pint of beer to the table, and James was surprised to see the young man had ordered himself a glass of orange juice.

Clicking glasses, James said, "Cheers, son, here's to our next big job."

"What next big job are you talking about?"

"Oh, aye, that's right, I've not mentioned it to you yet!"

After throwing the scotch over in one gulp, he continued, "I have this job lined up. It's not straightforward, but it's a good one. What we're going to do is…"

Seeing Peter's attention stray across the room, James said, "Are you listening? Or is your mind elsewhere?"

Still looking away, Peter said, "I'm listening, but I thought I recognized a guy at the bar."

"Friend or foe?"

"Foe, for sure," Peter replied nervously.

James glanced toward the bar. "Are you talking about him with the black coat?"

Peter nodded.

"Don't worry about that clown. I'll put him well out of your way."

"Do you know him?" asked Peter.

"Absolutely, I do. That's Pat Fallon, a fuckin' idiot, but give him his due, he has some good connections."

Peter went on to explain how he'd set him up in Spain.

Finding the story amusing, James said, "Don't bother your head about him. I'll have a word in his ear, and he'll never bother you again."

Just to prove his point, James called Fallon over to join them. "Pat, I've reason to believe you may want to discuss something with my young friend here, however, before you do, let me give you fair warning. If any harm comes to him, irrespective if you were involved or not, I promise I'll kill you."

Fallon stared at Peter. "No, James, I consider him one of you. He'll be okay."

James patted Fallon on the shoulder. "Thanks, Pat. Now that we have an understanding, let me buy you a drink."

Fallon made the excuse that he had some other business to take care off and wished James and Peter a pleasant night.

James said, "Now that Fallon's dealt with, let me tell you what I have going."

Feeling more relaxed, Peter was ready to jump through hoops for his mentor said sarcastically, "Okay, Reverend, let's hear it."

"Well, my boy, what I have in mind is no ordinary job—I think we should go into the antiques business."

The junior pickpocket looked puzzled. "I'm not sure what you mean...the antiques business?"

"Ask yourself who has antiques," James said. "Generally speaking, it's the wealthy bastards of this world, right?"

Nodding his head in agreement, the apprentice crook said, "Yes, I guess so."

Then the phony minister confidently replied, "Oh, there's no guesswork involved—it's a sure thing."

"So how do we get involved when we know absolutely nothing about antiques?" James stared into his empty glass. "Are you sure you don't want a pint or something a wee bit stronger?"

Peter thought about the effects of his last episode of drinking. "No thanks, James, but let me get you another one."

After further consideration, James said, "Perhaps you're right. I've had enough, so let me tell you my idea. We'll put adverts in local newspapers with words to this effect: International antiques dealer needs various pieces for the American market. Representatives will be in your area. Call for free valuation.'

"Now, young man, for the next few weeks we will study and familiarize ourselves with antiques, so when we call on people we'll sound as if we know what we're talking about."

Not really following James's train of thought, Peter asked, "What do we do when we visit the client?"

"Well, for starters, we'll be in their house. That gives us the opportunity to look around. One of us can talk the talk—you know, tell them their antiques are worth a fortune and get them excited. While that's happening, the other can pick up one or two bits and pieces. But, on the other hand, if we recognize something is of real value, we can perhaps make a killing on it."

Trying to convince himself James's idea would work, Peter said, "Okay, let's give it a go. At least it'll be something different."

26

COLLECTING ANTIQUES *can get old after a while.*

Overnight, the phone message for Saint Stevens Church Hampstead had miraculously changed to: Pendexter's International House of Antiques.

With business cards printed and adverts placed, the two Glaswegian antiques experts were ready to take their show on the road. However, if this game of charades was to succeed, it was imperative that they dressed the part. Both were fitted out with black pinstripe business suits, white shirts, conservative-looking ties, and well-polished shoes. And just for good measure, James wore a classy Gold Albert pocket watch taken from a city gent when he didn't realize he was being dispossessed of it.

The older of the dealers gave final instructions prior to reaching their first appointment. "Be polite and very professional. Try to lose a wee bit of the Scottish accent, and most of all, don't get flustered. Stay cool."

Before reaching the doorstep of what looked like a Victorian mansion, Peter said, "Aye, aye, Captain."

"Oh, do please come in, gentlemen. You are a little early and my son is running a tad late." The lady of the house welcomed them warmly. Giving good reason for her son's tardiness, she continued, "It's all due to his court case taking longer than expected. The Old Bailey is a very busy place these days. It would seem every second person is a crook."

Fluttering her hands, she asked, "Tea?"

When they declined, old lady added, "Who would want to be a government prosecutor? For the life of me, I don't know why he chose that profession."

The dealers looked at each other.

James checked his notepad to be sure he got the lady's name correct. "Mrs. Hawthorn, my partner and I have been inundated with enquiries. Rather than wait for your son, would you mind if we rescheduled your appointment?"

The innocent old woman said, "Are you sure? He shouldn't be much longer, however, if you wish to come back at a later date, that would be fine. It's times like this that I miss my dear husband. Jeffry always took care of these matters, but then again, he was a High Court judge and he, too, had a habit of running late."

The antiques dealers wished the lady a pleasant evening and exited the house as if it were on fire. As they walked away from the potential minefield, Peter said, "Thank God the prosecutor wasn't home—that could've been a very long appointment."

His counterpart said, "No kidding—like a minimum of ten years."

The positive Mr. Slavin then added, "There's one thing for sure, we'll never encounter a situation like that again."

As they continued their rapid departure from the judge's house, Peter said, "Where to next?"

James thumbed through his Pendexter's Antiques notepad.

"Here's a good one—a Mr. Woolfson. I remember chatting to him. He wants to sell everything and return to Germany."

Peter was still trying to shake off the ill effects of their first appointment and didn't sound overly enthusiastic, fearing they may have a similar experience.

Knocking on the Woolfson door several times, there was no sign of life. Then the door opened.

"Good evening, sir, we are from Pendexter International..."

Before Peter could get the word antique out, the man on the other side of the threshold, asked in very strong German accent, "Vi a yo ear?"

They repeated the introductions, but it was obvious the man was hard of hearing. The two antiquated hearing aids hanging from his balding head confirmed just how deaf their second client was.

After they'd raised their voices a few more decibels, the German finally understood and invited them in. Looking around the house, it was obvious the man didn't employ a housekeeper.

Still in a very raised tone, James asked, "What are you selling?"

The volume of the question suited the seller. "I'm gonna go ome. Am selling eva-ting. You boys wanna buy it? How much for eva-ting?"

As James was about to engage in a screaming conversation, Peter noticed a stack of gold coins sitting on an antique writing bureau. As he made his way towards the lot, the sharp old German said, "Ha, Mr., donna touch ma money."

Peter thought, *Right, it's game on. This guy's up for the challenge.*

Meanwhile, James was looking through all the guy's bits and pieces, asking the man a multitude of questions to give his accomplice time to search other parts of the house.

Peter then asked if he could use the bathroom.

"Sure, but I no have the toilet paper. I just use old newspapers—that's all they are good for these days."

Responding at an equal volume, Peter forgot his instructions of acting polished and said in a strong Glasgow accent, "No problem, I just need a piss."

The excursion to the bathroom was an ideal opportunity for the fingersmith to go to work. Urinating for a very short four seconds, he left the bathroom to quickly scan the surrounding rooms. Picking up pieces of jewelry and a few old gold watches that were lying on top of a dressing table, he made his way back to the living room.

Just before rejoining his partner, he noticed a briefcase on the floor. Pretending to bend down to tie his shoelace, he flicked it open. To his amazement, it contained envelopes stuffed with cash and old photos that looked like a young Mr. Woolfson in a German SS military uniform.

With one eye on the living room and one on the case, he spied an old German Luger pistol lying next to the cash. Conscious that the case shouldn't disturbed for the time being, he returned to join Mr. Woolfson and James in the living room.

Seeing the homeowner looking the other way, in a very low voice Peter asked his partner to divert the German's attention.

Walking toward the window on the other side of the room, James pointed to a piece of art which had never been hung on the wall. "Now, Mr. Woolfson, how much would you want for this painting here?"

As negotiations surrounding the piece of art took place, Peter moved out of sight of Woolfson and, picking up the briefcase, swiftly made his way toward the front door. Leaving the haul tucked in the hedge close to the heavy metal gate at the entrance to the front garden and hoping he hadn't been missed, Peter quickly returned to the room in time to hear James and the German negotiating a price for the work of art.

Giving James the nod, Peter said, "Mr. Woolfson, it's been a pleasure to meet a man of such extraordinary taste. I'll inform my office of everything you have for sale and my partner and I will be in touch."

The German began to cough, and Peter said, "We'll let ourselves out. Thank you and we wish you a very good evening."

As they left, closing the heavy door securely behind them, James had no idea what Peter had done, however, as they approached the front entrance, he saw the briefcase in the hedge.

Peter said, "Let's get moving. That old bastard will be calling the cops anytime now, but from the looks of what's in that case, I'm not sure what he'll report missing."

Returning to the apartment James had rented under the name of Richard Richardson, Peter emptied the contents of the night's work in the middle of the floor. They couldn't believe what spilled onto the worn carpet.

At the bottom of the case were gold dental fillings and an assortment of jewelry including diamond rings and earrings. It was obvious to the thieves that what lay in front of them was Woolfson's ill-gotten gains from his tour of duty in the German military.

Peter had never held a gun before—except for the toy water pistol he'd used on the Russians in Spain—and was reluctant to handle the German Luger.

The way James handled the weapon indicated he'd had lots experience in that particular department.

"Is it loaded?" inquired the rookie.

James checked. "Nope. The bastard probably emptied it into some poor Jew."

"How much do think is here?"

"I'm not sure," James said, "but all the notes look relatively new." He began to open the envelopes. After a few had been torn open, it was obvious there was nearly a quarter of a million pounds stashed in the bag.

Halfway through the counting Peter asked, "Do you think he'll catch us?"

James, the old campaigner, replied, "No, but we're not finished with our friend Mr. Woolfson."

"What do you mean? Don't tell me you want to go back there!"

"Listen, Peter, that guy may have called the cops and given them our description. If that's the case, we'll be looking over our shoulders for a long time to come. Now, if we show up unexpectedly on his doorstep—not dressed like a pair of toffs but like two guys intent on doing him damage—I have a sneaking suspicion he may want to listen to what we have to say."

"And what do we have to say?" Peter asked, curious.

James continued to count the money. "Let me sleep on that one."

At exactly one forty-five, the counting was complete—the evening's earnings amounted to two hundred and thirty-nine thousand pounds, plus the jewelry, and various pieces of gold and diamonds.

27

EARLY TO BED, *early to rise is okay if you have no friends.*

Their late night counting the spoils meant breakfast would not be a consideration, as both were catching up on a well-earned rest.

"Are you up for a nice lunch?" James asked his young partner.

"Absolutely! I'm hungry," replied the perky Peter. "And besides, we have a lot of talking to do."

"Yes, I've been thinking about that old bastard Woolfson—he's got to pay for his cruel deeds," said the angry pickpocketing pastor-now-antiques-dealer.

"James, don't you think it could be very risky going back there?"

"Of course, it's risky, but no riskier than many other things I've done."

Peter thought about the situation for a minute. "I think if we're going back to see him, we shouldn't harm him, but should threaten to expose him to those people...what are they called?"

"Do you mean the War Crimes Commission?" James asked.

"Yes, we'll tell him if he opens his mouth about us taking his money, we'll let the authorities know his whereabouts."

Smiling, Peter said, "We have evidence that would put him away for a very long time—perhaps forever."

Having enjoyed a first-class lunch, it was agreed that they should visit the former SS officer under cover of darkness.

This time the knock on the door was far from a gentle tap. Taking into consideration the anger they harbored toward the German and his lack of hearing, Peter almost kicked the door down.

Getting no response, James said, "Perhaps the bastard has gone back to Germany."

After trying several more times, there was still no movement on the other side of the large, weather-beaten, oak door.

James reached into his inside jacket pocket and produced a mini tool kit. After picking at the lock for no more than fifteen seconds, the door opened, and the pickpockets were on the other side ready to confront the man they held in total disdain.

The place was in darkness, but, familiar with the layout of the house, they switched on a light. Making their way toward the living room, they were shocked to see the lifeless body of Mr. Woolfson swinging from the main ceiling beam.

Startled, Peter said, "Holy fuck! Let's get out of here!"

"Hold your horses. Let's have a look around—perhaps there's more to collect."

"Listen, we already have plenty—we don't need anything else. Please, let's go! The cops could turn up any time—then we're done for."

"Okay, but let me check just one more thing."

On their previous visit, James remembered a piece of furniture that had sat beside the fireplace—it was no longer there. Upon further inspection, he noticed it had been moved toward the window. It was a very simple piece, but what drew his attention was a small, locked drawer.

Taking a penknife from his mini tool kit, he forced the drawer open to find an array of spectacular diamonds and precious stones. Looking to Peter, he said, "I knew something decent had to be in that drawer. Now let's go."

Peter showed no interest in the find—his only objective was to get away from the German swinging from the ceiling beam.

Nearing James's apartment, they could see some unfamiliar cars parked nearby and what looked to be undercover police officers. James instructed his protege to keep walking and not to look at them. He handed Peter the small black velvet pouch with the precious stones.

From out of nowhere, four or five officers emerged.

James said, "Run, son, I'll take care of them."

The pickpocket didn't hesitate. He took off like an Olympic sprinter, only turning for a second to see James ambushed by what looked to be every policeman in London.

As he ran, he thanked God he hadn't left his cut of the money in James's apartment.

The wealth the youthful pickpocket had accumulated was beyond his wildest dreams—he lacked for nothing, yet there still seemed to be a void.

In Peter Cooney's mind, what was yet to be fulfilled and had been missing all his life, was to be recognized as a true and worthwhile member of society.

From his days in the Glasgow orphanage through leaving school in Kent, it had been drummed into him that he was useless, that he wouldn't amount to anything. Now financially secure and in a position to prove the world wrong, he decided his days of slipping his hands into people's pockets were gone forever.

Having dinner with an attractive young lady he'd met when taking a night class studying Spanish, he lent an ear to the waiter politely bending down to whisper, "Sir, there is a man standing at the lectern who said you know him. He would like word."

Peter excused himself and as he made his way across the room, he recognized the man instantly. It was the notorious Pat Fallon.

The now-ex-pickpocket smiled and said, "Mr. Fallon, what is it going to take to get rid of you?"

Fallon answered in a very matter-of-fact tone. "James will be released next week. Meet him outside Harrods on Tuesday at three o'clock."

After delivering the message, and not looking comfortable in the surroundings of the upscale eatery, Fallon turned and quickly exited the premises.

He returned to his table and said, "Sorry about the interruption, my dear."

"Is everything okay, Peter? You've gone a little pale," said the lady who was becoming very fond of the now more sophisticated Peter Cooney.

"I'm fine. It was a friend who knows I frequent this restaurant—he thought he'd call to tell me he can't make our appointment tomorrow. It's no big deal."

For Peter, Tuesday couldn't come quick enough. It had been three years since that fateful night when he'd sprinted away, leaving his accomplice to face the music with the undercover detectives.

While waiting for the man who had taken the rap for the robbery at the commandant's house, Peter was caught off guard when a very thin and much older-looking James Slavin tapped him on the shoulder.

"How you doin', son? Life treating you okay?"

Before Peter could strike up a conversation, he was ushered away by a few large gentlemen.

Sitting in the rear seat with the man who'd spent the last three years in the nick for their activities, Peter said, "You're looking well, James."

"Don't give me that shit. I have plenty of mirrors at home and I know exactly how I look. However, I have a question for you. Where are the stones?"

Anticipating that Slavin would ask him for the little black bag, he reached into his pocket and handed it over. "They're all there—just as you gave them to me. I won't even charge you a storage fee."

He smiled and added, "I was thinking about using the large diamond for a wedding ring but couldn't find a woman deserving of it."

Peter's unexpected actions left Slavin speechless. Finally, finding his voice, he said, "I must be honest with you, son, I never expected you to show up today, and certainly never thought I'd see those stones again."

Although Peter may not have been in the safest of environments, he displayed tremendous fortitude. "Listen, James, perhaps you're used to dealing with arse-holes, but I'm not one of them. Now, tell your minders to take a walk. You can meet up with them where they so politely invited me into the car. Oh, and by the way, whatever cash I got from that German bastard is mine, do you hear me? It's mine! I don't want your heavy-handed friends chasing after me for what belongs to me. Deal?"

Sighing deeply, James nodded. "It's a deal."

Having returned to where the little excursion began, Peter shook James's hand and gave him a bear hug, reaching into the unsuspecting ex-pastor's pocket at the same time. He retrieved the little black bag of precious stones in one fluid motion.

"James, it was a real pleasure getting to know you, however, with respect, we can never be partners. I've only had one partner and he's dead. I wish you well, my friend. Take care."

Peter left the car and never looked back.

28

"VOY A COMPRAR una granja."

After repeating this over and over in Spanish, which translates to, "I'm going to buy a farm", the pickpocket was determined to carry out what was fast becoming his dream. And having the resources, the dream was fast becoming a reality.

"What's the name of that song you're constantly singing?" asked Maggie, his friend from the Monday evening Spanish class.

"The Farmer Wants a Wife."

Secretly, it wasn't just the farmer who wanted a wife—it was the pickpocket who wanted Maggie to be his wife.

There were only two more classes remaining and the course would be finished. Then it would be, "Hasta la vista, baby."

Peter knew if the farmer really wanted that wife, he had to make a move, and make it soon. Remembering one young lady who had referred to him as a bullfighter, he now realized he would require the courage of a matador if he really wanted to secure Maggie's hand in marriage.

The evening of the final class, the former pickpocket was preoccupied with matters far greater than learning how to converse with the butcher, the baker, and the candlestick maker in Barcelona.

Forget Spanish! He wanted to find the appropriate words in English to ask Maggie to marry him. Planning the perfect opportunity to pop the question was his first task. He made reservations at a nice quiet Spanish restaurant near Portobello Road in the city.

He literally left no stone unturned. The engagement ring was nothing short of spectacular: it featured a very large diamond and the gold band was encrusted with a multitude of precious stones—the jewels were supplied by some old German SS officer.

After rehearsing the question over and over in his mind, the man who prided himself on his forthrightness struggled to say what he wanted most. Biting the bullet, he asked, "Maggie, how would you like to go for a bite after class tonight?"

"Peter, that is so thoughtful. I'd love to."

The pickpocket was relieved his invitation was met with such enthusiasm. "I thought I'd reserve a table at Pablo's Cantina."

Excited, Maggie said, "I love Spanish food! In fact, it's my dream to someday live in Spain—I love the country."

The pickpocket thought he was dreaming as all the appropriate boxes were rapidly being ticked. As they sat enjoying the Spanish cuisine and making small talk, the would-be farmer knew it was make-or-break time.

Taking a deep breath, he said, "Maggie, voy a comprar una granja."

Puzzled, Maggie said, "Peter, I've only been in the Spanish class for six weeks. Please tell me what you're saying."

"It means I'm going to buy a farm in Spain, and I want you to be my wife. You've heard me sing 'The Farmer Wants a Wife.' Well, will you be the farmer's wife?"

There was a deadly silence, and then Maggie said, "What you said in Spanish didn't sound like you were asking me to marry you."

On a roll, the pickpocket said, "Never mind the Spanish, Maggie, will you marry me?"

The young lady began to cry. "Yes, but there's something I want to tell you. And after you hear it, you may have second thoughts."

Having no clue what was coming next, Peter braced himself for something devastating. "Okay, let's hear it."

"I'll get straight to the point," she sniffled. "I have a history of shoplifting and recently I was caught. I'm so ashamed of myself. I don't know why I did such a thing, but if you'll still accept me, I'd love to be a farmer's wife."

He smiled. "Oh, Maggie, I'm not sure if I could marry a person who has stolen something, but then again, I suppose if I told you I'd stolen one or two things in the past, I'm sure you'd still marry me."

Taking Peter's hand, Maggie said, "Of course, I would."

Then Peter asked a curious question. "What's that box in your coat pocket?"

Having no idea what he was talking about, she reached behind her chair and pulled a little gift box from her raincoat. When she opened it, her eyes glistened with unshed tears. "Oh, my God, Peter, it's so beautiful! Where did you get such a beautiful ring?"

"I stole it."

As Maggie laughed, he slipped the ring on her finger. "Maggie Dawson, I love you."

Delighted with the way the night was progressing, Peter said, "Darling, I'm serious—I really want to buy a small farm in Spain and spend the rest of my life there. And now that I'll have a beautiful wife to help me, I want to go as soon as possible."

"I've heard of house-hunting, but never farm-hunting, especially in Spain." Then, she hesitated. "Wait a minute. My cousin is in real estate and she deals with international properties. I'll ask her to do some research for us. But, Peter, there's just one little problem—how are we going to afford to buy a farm in Spain? It'll be so expensive."

Peter smiled. "Where there's a will, there's a way."

As positive as Peter sounded, Maggie wanted to bring him down to earth. "It all sounds lovely, but seriously, a farm would cost a fortune."

"Please do me a huge favor and speak with your cousin. Leave the cost of it to me. I'm sure we'll get the money from somewhere."

The following day, Peter was hoping Maggie's cousin had researched some Spanish farm properties they could consider viewing. However, the call he received wasn't good news.

Maggie informed him she'd had second thoughts about living the life of a farmer's wife in Spain and wanted to call the whole thing off.

"But why?"

"If you really want to know, have a look at the front page of this morning's newspaper." Then, she hung up.

Having no idea what she was talking about, he instantly ran from his apartment to the local news agents. There it was, a photo of his face spread across the front page. The headlines read, "Peter Patrick Cooney—the most wanted jewel thief in Britain."

He bolted from the shop in the event someone may recognize him from the article. Packing his bag to get out of town, he pondered what would cause him to gain such notoriety. The answer hit him immediately. *James Slavin--the bastard has set me up.*

The move he'd made with the bag of jewels in the rear of the car had come back to haunt him.

In his excitement, he missed a telephone call. The caller left a message. "You seem to be quite a popular man, Mr. Cooney. I see you made the front pages. I wonder if anyone has recognized you? Your greed is going to cost you big time, young man."

The call confirmed the pickpocket's suspicions—Slavin was coming after him. How to outwit the con-man? Was it going to be a game of cat and mouse? Or was he going to go on the offensive? In the meantime, the various strategies had to be put on hold—the first priority was finding a safe place to lay low until things cooled down.

Traveling light wasn't a problem—he was conditioned to living a nomadic lifestyle. *I'll move up to Scotland,* he thought, then remembered his friend Danny Wilson who had helped him with his exodus from the land of his birth.

He hadn't been in touch with Danny for years and wondered if he still worked as a chef. Racking his brain trying to remember the name of the five-star hotel where he first started working, it came back to him.

"The Dorchester," he said out loud. "That's where he worked. I'm positive it was the Dorchester."

Walking through London wearing sunglasses and a baseball cap, he thought every person on the streets of London had bought the morning paper and was on the lookout for a master jewel thief.

Standing outside one the most prestigious hotels in the country, he made the call. "Good morning. Could I speak to chef Danny Wilson, please?"

The very polite telephone receptionist said, "Please hold the line and I'll transfer you to our culinary department."

Waiting to be put through felt like an eternity, then a male voice said, "Kitchen, how can I help you?"

Nervously, the pickpocket said, "Could I speak with Danny Wilson, please?"

"Head Chef Wilson is occupied at present. Can I give him a message?"

"No, that's okay, I'll try again later."

Missing out on breakfast due to the headlines, Peter thought he'd get some lunch. As he gulped it down, he was thinking when he got in touch with his friend Danny he'd ask him to prepare one of those fancy dinners for him.

The next call was put straight through. Sounding a little desperate, he said, "Danny? Is that you, Danny?"

A very polished English accent answered, "Who is this?"

"It's me, Peter, Peter Cooney."

The chef's voice dropped to a whisper. "For fuck's sake, Peter, what have you done? You're all over the newspapers, mate. Where are you?"

Delighted to hear Danny's caring tone, Peter replied, "I'm outside the place you're working. I'm in a wee bit of trouble and I need to see you, pal."

"You'll have to hang about for another hour. I finish early today—I'll see you at two thirty. Can you see that wee cafe on the corner across the road from the hotel?"

Peter looked around. "Yes, I see it."

"I'll meet you there at two thirty."

Looking into his cup and seeing the dregs of the third refill of Earl Grey, he began to wonder what was causing Danny's delay. Was the chef having second thoughts about reuniting with his pal from the orphanage?

Checking his watch to see if it was synchronized with the café's wall clock, he noted that they were both in harmony.

At that moment, in he came. This wasn't the same Danny Wilson he'd known all those years ago. This guy was at least three hundred pounds.

"Danny, I'm over here!" Peter shouted to capture his friend's attention.

Danny gave Peter a hug that just about crushed him. "My God, Peter, it's great to see you. You haven't changed a bit."

Peter glibly responded, "For fuck's sake, Danny, you've put on a bit of weight. Does anybody get fed in that hotel or do you eat all the grub before it gets to them?"

The chef laughed. "I'm obligated to taste whatever I cook—it's one of the perks of the job."

His demeanor changed. "Anyway, what in God's name have you been up to? When I saw your picture in the paper, I couldn't believe it was you. Tell me, what's going on?"

Finishing off what was left of his now-cold tea, Peter said, "I'll tell you everything, but it'll take a while. First, though, I need a place where I can lay low for a few days, you know, just to let things cool down."

Danny cupped his face in his large hands and said, "Peter, things are different for me now. I'm married and have two wee boys."

Then the chef pulled out what looked like a miniature family album. Pointing to a picture of two little West Indian children, he said, "That's Nick and Peter. Believe it or not, I named Peter after you."

"Who's the lady?" Peter asked.

Proudly, Danny said, "That's my wife. Her name's Margaret Anne."

Observing his friend staring hard at the picture, Danny asked, "What's wrong? What are you staring at?"

Peter was of two minds as to whether to comment or not. "Danny, she is really b-beautiful."

Not mincing his words, his friend said, "You were going to say she's black! Well, Peter, she *is* black and you're correct—she's very beautiful. She has given me two wonderful boys."

Peter recognized the pride Danny had for his wife and children. "You've come a long way. You seem to have it all together and I'm really pleased for you. Now, big Danny Wilson has a good steady job, a nice wife, and kids. You've done well, pal."

Cutting through all the patronization, Danny said, "Okay, Peter, what do you need me to do for you?"

Hearing his friend reaching out, Peter became emotional. Trying to regain his composure, he said, "I'm in the shit, Danny. I have the hounds chasing me and they're coming from all angles. I just need to be in a safe place for three or four days."

In his usual caring manner, Danny said, "First of all, do you need some cash?"

"No, pal, money is the least of my concerns. In fact, I can give you some. As I say, I just need to be somewhere that I can be out of harm's way."

To Peter's relief, Danny said, "Don't worry, I've got the perfect place for you, but first let me make a phone call."

Within minutes, Danny returned. "It's taken care of, but you'll have to keep yourself to yourself—don't advertise what you've been up to. You know how it works."

Peter breathed a sigh of relief. "No problem. When can we go?"

Aware he was helping his pal, Danny smiled and said, "We're on our way. Let's go."

29

WHEN YOU'VE HAD enough, it may be time to bluff.

"Danny, where we going? You've been driving almost an hour and a half."

"Don't you worry, my wee Glasgow pal, we'll soon be there. I'm taking you to a spot where no one will find you."

When Danny eventually stopped the car, the pickpocket thought he was having a moment of déjà vu, but this time it wasn't a Spanish farmhouse. This one was in the heart of the English countryside.

Grabbing his very light luggage, the fugitive followed his guardian angel to what could only be described as the smallest farmhouse in England.

Performing the formal introductions, Danny said, "Peter, I'd like to introduce you to my two wonderful friends, Mr. and Mrs. Adams."

Peter shook their hands and Danny went on to say, "They're aware that you're a very popular man—they saw your picture in the paper—but don't worry. You're safe here."

Embarrassed at the way Danny had introduced him, Peter said, "Mr. and Mrs. Adams, I promise I'll be on my best behavior."

"Oh, I'm not worried, son," the old farmer said. "If you start any funny games, I'll blow your head off. Your friend Danny will tell you that I'm for real, and more than capable, so we'll just leave it at that."

Peter thought to himself, *It's times like these I need that toy water pistol.*

Happy to be in a safe environment, he thanked the old couple for their hospitality.

Danny checked his watch. "Okay, if I'm going to beat the rush hour traffic, I'd better get moving. I'll check in with you in a couple of days."

As the knight in shining armor drove off, old Mrs. Adams showed the lodger where he'd be sleeping until things cooled down.

At the end of a small passageway leading toward the back door of the house, there was a wall panel that the farmer's wife pushed. "I hope you'll be comfy down here. It's a nice quiet part of the house and if we do get any unexpected guests, you'll never be found."

Just before Mrs. Adams walked away, she said, "Pay no attention to my Harry. He just wants to protect me. And, by the way, your friend Danny saved my son Tommy's life, so know you'll be all right with us."

Giving her guest a motherly hug, Mrs. Adams went back to join her husband.

The following morning, the concerned old lady knocked on the wall. "Are you all right in there?"

Concerned that Peter hadn't come for breakfast and getting no response to her call, she opened the secret wall panel to find the room empty. Upon further inspection she found a handwritten note by the bed.

"Dear Mr. and Mrs. Adams, I'd like to thank you for your kindness and hospitality. I'm sorry I left without saying goodbye, but I had to leave urgently. I'll explain later, if I'm still alive. Peter."

As soon as Mrs. Adams read the note, she shouted, "Harry! Harry! Come quick. The young fellow has gone."

Hearing his wife upset, the agile old farmer ran to see if the pickpocket was still on the property, but the lodger was nowhere to be seen.

"Mary, there's no sign of him in the yard."

The elderly couple knew they couldn't phone the police, but they tried calling Danny—his phone went straight to voice mail.

"Where could he be?" the elderly couple wondered.

Meanwhile, Peter was on his way to see Maggie, the shoplifter who had rejected his marriage proposal. He had received a disturbing call from her, precipitating his immediate departure from the farm.

"Peter, a man called me saying if I don't contact him before two this afternoon, he's going to kill you."

She was amazed at how calm Peter was about her frightful predicament.

As she held the pickpocket's hand, he said, "I'll take care of the bastard, but you must promise me after it's done, you'll at least hear what I have to say. I'm not the monster you may think I am."

Holding on even tighter, Maggie said, "If I thought you were a monster, I wouldn't have called you. I've not stopped thinking about you, so please tell me you're going to be okay. I really want to be a farmer's wife, but it must be in Spain."

Peter gave his wife-to-be the most passionate kiss she had ever had in her life, and then told her the plan he had to put Slavin away once and for all.

"Maggie, call the guy and tell him you'll meet him on one condition—that he comes alone. If he agrees, tell him to meet you at the teahouse next to Finsbury Park underground station. It's next door to the police station."

She made the call, but Slavin didn't agree to the meeting location—he wanted to meet somewhere in his neck of the woods. Peter was monitoring the call and signaled to Maggie the deal was off. But within minutes, the con man called back and agreed to her terms.

"Now what?" she asked nervously.

Peter said, "You'll be in the tea room waiting for him. As soon he sits down, it will become a table for three. When I give you the signal, say you're going to use the ladies' room, then leave the shop as quickly as you can. Don't hang around outside—go straight to your apartment. I'll meet you there later."

"But..."

"Maggie, you've got to trust me. I'm going to make it happen for us—I desperately want that Spanish farm, also."

At fifteen minutes before two, Maggie's hand was shaking as she tried to steady a hot cup of tea. Then, true to form, James Slavin boldly sat down without asking.

Much to his surprise, Peter joined them. "What a coincidence, James, I didn't think you liked tea."

Peter adjusted his baseball cap and Maggie knew that was her signal.

"Excuse me, gentlemen, I have to use the ladies' room."

As Maggie rose from the chair, Peter stood to pull it out for her.

Simultaneously, Slavin stood.

As soon as Maggie was out of earshot, Peter said, "I didn't authorize you to go anywhere, arse-hole. Sit down."

Peter's words took Slavin by surprise and he obeyed the instruction. Using the same tactics he'd used on the horse expert months earlier, he said, "Now, James, my good man, the ball is back in my court. If you're wondering what I'm talking about, let me explain. You see, that little bag of jewels I took from you is going to pay for having you shot."

Slavin began to smirk. As he started to stand, Peter said, "Before you think about leaving, you should know there are three guys waiting for you outside. You could phone some of your heavies...you know, those arse-holes that hang around you, but that may prove to be a problem as your phone is in my friend's bag and it may be some time before she returns from the toilet. In fact, there's a good chance she isn't even in the building."

Peter glanced over Slavin's shoulder. "If you turn around very slowly, you'll see a man with a newspaper held up to his face. He is also holding a gun that will end your life if you try any of your smart moves."

The con man succumbed to the pickpocket's advice. "Okay, what's the deal, smart guy?"

"Oh, there is no deal for you, James. Your threatening phone calls prevented that."

Slavin realized the pickpocket was for real and began to get fidgety. "Come on, Peter. I'm sure we can come to some arrangement."

Still remaining cool as a cucumber, Peter said, "James, you've not been listening. There is no deal and there is no arrangement." Then, appearing to have a change of heart, Peter said, "All right, I'll tell you what I'll do. I'll let you off the hook on one condition. When you leave here, you'll walk into the police station across the street and tell them you made false allegations against me. Also, you'll have all that shit in the newspapers taken care of—tell them it was a big mistake."

Now on a roll, he continued, "I know there's a very good chance you'll not do any of the things I've asked. Well, that's okay, also, as I've already paid a fifty percent deposit to have you blown away. So, if you want to take the chance, Pastor Pendexter, you feel free to do so."

Once again, the pickpocket's bluff paid off.

***

Having the day off, Danny ate a leisurely breakfast and then opened the morning paper. There it was in black and white, a public apology. The article read: "This newspaper has been misinformed and wishes to publicly apologize to Mr. Peter Patrick Cooney for our slanderous report regarding his honesty and integrity."

Danny smiled. "I don't know how you did it, pal, but you did it."

The real praise, though, came from the lady who was counting the days until she was with her Spanish farmer.

Now that Slavin was out of the picture, the pickpocket was, in every sense of the word, ready to move on to pastures new, and begin life as a Spanish farmer.

Maggie's cousin had located the ideal spot, a prime piece of property in southern Spain which was within the pickpocket's budget.

Prior to taking the big step, the enthusiastic couple decided it would be wise to spend a week in the nearby village where they would soon become the newest residents. Immediately after their arrival, they knew they had found the place where they wanted to be. The tranquil setting and the friendliness of the locals convinced them this would be their happy-ever-after land.

On their return, they agreed Maggie would go in advance, allowing Peter to finalize any bits and pieces of business that had to be taken care of.

Then the big day finally arrived. Making his way through Heathrow airport, traveling light with only one piece of hand luggage, he was set to collect his boarding pass for the three-hour flight to Barcelona, when he was approached by a man in a navy-blue raincoat.

"Excuse me, sir, are you Mr. Peter Cooney?"

The gentleman flashed an ID card in front of his face. "My name is Chief Inspector Charles Frazer of the City of London Serious Crimes Unit."

Before Peter could respond to the policeman's question, he was advised that he was under arrest in connection with a major bank robbery."

Caught completely by surprise, he answered, "I think you're talking to the wrong Peter Cooney. There must be a million of us out there."

The inspector said, "That may be the case, sir, but it would appear you match the description of the Peter Cooney we're looking for."

The pickpocket smiled, appreciating the Chief Inspector's humor. "Inspector, everyone has a double—maybe you should be looking for guy that looks like me."

He was then asked to escort the Chief Inspector to a waiting police car. He disobeyed the inspector's request, opting to obey his inner voice and took off like a gazelle, apologizing to travelers as he bumped into them with his hand luggage.

This escape from the police wasn't the pickpocket's first rodeo. It had become second nature to him, but on this occasion, it seemed different. He scampered out of sight of the uniformed officers who relinquished the chase due to the pickpocket's superior athleticism. Continuing to pick up the pace, his focus was not on escaping incarceration, but on joining the woman he loved.

Initially, he'd been looking at a two-and-a-half-hour flight to be reunited with the farmer's wife-in-waiting. However, after his unexpected meeting with the Chief Inspector, and the subsequent effect it had on his itinerary, his relocating to Spain was looking more like a two-and-a-half-week land-and-sea excursion.

After explaining to his sweetheart that he would be delayed, organizing new travel plans was his next priority. He envisioned his mug shot being displayed at every seaport around the British Isles, so he made arrangements to be ferried to France on a fishing trawler.

The cost of the midnight voyage could've covered several return flights from London to Barcelona, however, paying the additional premium ensured there would be no further delays. Ten years in an English prison came to mind.

Although he had still to join Maggie, journeying through France via road and rail was enjoyable, knowing he wouldn't have to look over his shoulder—his crimes didn't merit the attention of Interpol.

On his travels, there were many occasions when he was tempted to ply his trade, however, he opted to stay on the straight and narrow, eliminating the risk of being caught in the act, which would've resulted in even more delays.

30

WHEN YOU FIND IT difficult to teach an old dog new tricks, a goldfish may be a good option.

As he approached the hacienda, he hoped the southern Spanish farm would complete his "happy ever after story." Looking around, he couldn't believe just how wonderful the place was. Closing his eyes, he murmured, "Thank you, Jesus." He was then met by a tearful Maggie.

Running into his arms, she said, "Oh, darling, I thought you'd never come!"

Hearing the relief and joy in his lover's voice, he caressed her and whispered, "Maggie, I've missed you so much, but I'm here to stay."

She shared his passionate embrace. "Oh, I've missed you more than words can say, but I've lots to tell you."

Taking a deep breath, she began to update her lover on the happenings of farm life in his absence. "Molly, the big gray cow that looks more like an elephant, had a calf, and five of our chickens were stolen or ran away. All I know is, we only have seven left. Francisco, our neighbor, said there are lots of foxes that could have eaten them, but my guess is, there are lots of two-legged foxes around these parts."

"Slow down, darling, I'll hear all about it, but first, can we go into the house?"

Peter couldn't believe how well Maggie had settled into her new environment—this was a million miles from the hustle and bustle of the streets of London.

"Close your eyes, Maggie, I've something for you!" The pickpocket pulled a small box from his luggage. When he put it into her hand, she opened her eyes.

"What is it?" Then she gave him a stern look. "Please don't tell me you stole it! You promised you'd never do that kind of thing again."

In an even stronger reprimanding tone, Peter said, "Listen, Maggie, when I gave you my word that I would never pick another pocket, I meant what I said. Now, please open the box."

Maggie knew her lover was upset by her glib remark and quickly apologized. "I'm sorry, my darling, I just don't want you to get caught and be taken away from me."

"Apology accepted. Now, open it."

Having no idea what the little box might contain, she lifted the lid very cautiously. "Oh, it's so beautiful! Are they real diamonds?"

Exchanging his Scottish accent for a strong cockney market trader twang, he said, "Noting but the best fer me Duchess!" Then reverting to his west of Scotland accent, he said, "Of course, they're real. I wouldn't have the one I love wearing any fake stones."

Smiling he added, "Maggie, my darling, only the best for the best!"

Slipping the massive ring over her pointer finger, she said, "How many rings can a farmer's wife wear?"

He laughed. "Not too many when there are so many cows to be milked!" Continuing, he said, "All this jewelry may come in handy someday if things get tight—at least you'll have something to get you through tough times."

Not being a materialistic girl, Maggie appreciated the pickpocket's wisdom. "My dad used to say, 'You never miss the water until the well runs dry.'"

Peter nodded in approval of her father's wisdom, but in reality, he hadn't a clue what she was talking about. However, he knew if they ever encountered a recessive period, they wouldn't be without food to put on the hundred-year-old farmhouse table.

Adjusting to his new occupation took several weeks if not months. Being a creature of habit, he never looked forward to breakfast before eight, so meeting the day any earlier was extremely challenging. The early rise he could just about tolerate but tending to livestock at such an ungodly hour he adjudged a detestable chore.

Every morning as he swung his legs out of bed, he would always lean over to the warm and cozy body of his helper. "Maggie, one day I'll have someone to do this for us."

His complaint would always be met with the same reply. "I know, darling, but until such times, please try not to make too much noise as you leave."

On his way to the cattle shed, he began to appreciate the advantages of the early rise and the tranquility the early morning offered, especially seeing the sun rise over the nearby mountains.

As laborious as his start to the day may have been, the pickpocket was grateful for the companionship of his canine friend, Tully. He knew the dog and his master shared a commonality—they were two Scottish terriers, albeit one had four legs and the other two.

After he had tended to the cattle, another advantage of the early rise was it promoted a great appetite for breakfast. Tully would race ahead to give Maggie due notice that her hungry partner was fast approaching. That gave her the opportunity to have the bacon and eggs on the table.

The dog's efforts didn't go unrewarded. He would sit at his master's feet enjoying his share of the crispy bacon.

After a year or so, the morning ritual came to a crashing halt when Maggie informed her soul-mate she was experiencing chest pains. The ever-caring Peter whisked her off to see the local doctor.

After the physician examined the happy-go-lucky lady of the farm, he referred her to a specialist at the general hospital in Barcelona. It was there the love of his life was diagnosed with an incurable cancer. The pickpocket tried to remain positive, praying Maggie would make a miraculous recovery.

Unfortunately, it wasn't to be. The youthful Maggie's condition deteriorated at a rapid pace. From her initial visit with the local doctor in town to within seven weeks in the city hospital, Peter kissed Maggie's forehead for the final time, and said goodbye to the one true love of his life.

Peter-the-pickpocket's existence had taken a drastic change. Where before, working on the farm was his passion, but having lost his soul-mate and his will to live, he decided to sell.

After many months of contemplation and uncertainty, the retired professional pickpocket decided to return to the land of his birth. The two questions that occupied his tortured mind were "Why did she have to die?" and "What am I going to do next?"

Like everything else in the pickpocket's life, opportunities presented themselves at the least expected times, and what lay ahead would prove no exception.

After returning to London, Peter decided to take the train from London's Kings Cross and travel up to Scotland. This was a return journey that held many memories. As the new and improved locomotive sped its way to the country of his birth, the pickpocket reminisced about the journey he'd made south all those years ago.

Arriving at Glasgow central and exiting the station, he felt a tug on his arm. "Peter, you probably don't recognize me—I'm Sean McCoy. I was in the orphanage with you."

The pickpocket could not confirm the stranger's allegations. "I'm sorry, pal, I don't remember you. I haven't a clue who you are. How did you recognize me?"

McCoy said, "Apart from your striking good looks, it's that confident swagger you have. You had the same swagger when you were a kid."

Enjoying the stranger's complimentary remarks, Peter suggested they go for a pint or two and rekindle old times—a distant past the pickpocket had hoped never to revisit.

The couple of pints quickly graduated to a level that could be best described as a bucket load. Over the course of the evening, the pickpocket's new best friend uncovered many happenings that his drinking pal had long since forgotten or chosen not to remember.

McCoy's photographic recall projected hurtful images of circumstances that caused Peter a certain discomfort. But there were parts of the conversation that both men found funny, promoting uncontrollable bouts of laughter.

Toward the end of evening, after a multitude of topics had been addressed, some of which they agreed upon and others on which they locked horns, there was one area where they discovered a shared commonality. Despite their humble beginnings, they recognized each had an insatiable appetite for the finer things in life.

However, there was an ethical wedge separating the former orphanage boys. One had worked his ass off to achieve the lifestyle befitting the upper class, where the other stole to get what he wanted.

So, when the subject of occupations arose, McCoy didn't hesitate, proudly stating that he had overcome his humble beginnings and now headed his own thriving law practice.

"What about your good self, Peter? What are you up to these days?"

The pickpocket felt reluctant to divulge what he'd been doing since making the great escape from the high walls of the prison-like orphanage. "Nothing too exciting, Sean. You know, a wee bit of this and that."

Taking a large gulp of his dark beer, McCoy put his courtroom skills to work and began to cross examine the professional fingersmith.

"A wee bit of this and that... Hm... I think you're keeping your cards close to your chest, my good friend. Something tells me you've been up to no good."

Sensing an element of disrespect in the lawyer's inquiring tone, the pickpocket met his accuser with an equal amount of brashness. "Sean, I'm here for a pint, I'm not on fuckin' trial, so stop being a nosy bastard. I'm not telling you what I've been doing for the past twenty odd years, however, I'm pleased you're doing well. But rest assured I'll never be in need of your professional services."

The pickpocket's reply put the lawyer in a position where he had a choice—either change the subject or go home to his wife and two lovely kids.

After being spoon fed with a few little snippets of Peter Cooney's intriguing past, the lawyer was only too happy to remain in the company of his very interesting friend. As they clicked glasses for the final drink of the evening, McCoy asked Peter if they could meet up some time soon.

"Perhaps I'll see you in court. Until then, you take care."

***

Being back in the city of his birth, many of the surroundings looked unrecognizable, yet there was an element of familiarity that stirred homesick emotions. Lying on top of his city center hotel bed, Peter began to question the wisdom of returning to the place he'd fled all those years ago.

What am I doing here? And what am I going to do now?

It was at breakfast the following morning that he got the unexpected answer to the questions.

Looking out the hotel dining room window, he happened to notice a truck parked outside the bank across the road, either delivering money or collecting it.

In only moments, he realized he was witnessing a robbery—and a very messy robbery it was.

The question ran through his mind: "Would I like to be on the side of the robbers? Or on the side of the men whose job it was to guard the money?"

After three seconds, he concluded he would go for the cash.

There was an extreme lack of professionalism, both on the part of the robbers and the security firm. Immediately leaving his breakfast, Peter dashed across the road to the scene, hoping to lend his expertise to the fumbling and woefully inadequate robbers. However, in his mind, he heard the voice of his late wife saying, "Peter, promise me you'll never pick pockets or steal from anyone again."

His steps slowed. *Should I help the guards or the masked gang?*

His love for Maggie won and he shouted, "What the hell are you guys doing? My brother is the manager here and he only has three months until retirement!"

A heavy Glasgow accent answered him. "Get yourself out of there or we'll take you and your damned brother both out. We only want the money!"

Never one to turn his back on a challenge, it was now "game on." Peter directed his comments to the man with the loud mouth and the sawed-off shotgun.

"Okay, ya big cowardly bastard, fire yer gun or I'll stick it up yer arse!"

Peter was shocked to hear a familiar voice.

"It's me, Peter, Sean McCoy. Hold yer horses."

The pickpocket couldn't believe his ears. Only two nights earlier, this same guy had boasted of having his own law firm—now he's robbing a bank?

"Sean? What the hell is going on? Are you a damned bank robber or a lawyer? You and your pals get yourselves outta here. Go!"

McCoy and his band of thieves made a run for it, allowing the guards to regain possession of the cash.

Much to Peter's surprise, the robbery claimed precedence in the television evening news, the leading story on every channel. He appeared to be the man who'd saved the day, but in his mind, the replay fueled his belief that given the proper circumstances, he would've done a much better job of robbing the bank than McCoy and the others who'd messed it up.

Then flashes of the promises he'd made to his darling Maggie ran through his mind...that he would never return to a life of crime.

It was at that point in the internal debate that he concluded he would turn his life around and do the opposite of that which he felt inclined. For the pickpocket it was "poacher turned gamekeeper."

After permitting one interview in which he adamantly stated he would be working with the city youth to try and reduce the number of young lives heading into a life of crime, he avoided the reporters wanting to speak with the hero of the hour.

The next evening, as he tried to sneak out the back door of the hotel, Sean McCoy caught up to him.

"Mr. Cooney, could I possibly have a word with you?"

Peter turned to see the elusive lawyer/robber and invited him to the hotel bar, anxious to hear his story. But this time, it was *his* turn to cross examine the man who had pretended to be a big-shot attorney.

Clicking glasses for the first pint of the day, Peter asked, "Who are you? Is Sean even your real name?"

"Oh, that's my name, Mr. Hero-of-Bank-Robbery fame. Had you just left me alone, you never would've seen me again, but since you involved yourself, it's made things a bit awkward. The guys who were working the bank job want to take you out."

Silence fell between them as the threat hung heavy in the air.

Peter grew agitated. "I'm not sure what you've been doing since the days in the orphanage, Sean, but let me tell you a little secret. I've been up to no good myself, but I'm done with that life. If you or your cronies want to come after me, you know where to find me."

McCoy back-tracked. "No, Peter, I'm not here to deliver a threat. I heard your interview and I know you want to help kids get on the straight and narrow. I want to be involved, too. I'm tired of the stupid stuff I've been doing over the years. Let me help."

Peter was wary of McCoy's offer but was willing to forego his doubts and take him aboard. After all, if *he* could change, why couldn't Sean?

Unlike their previous drinking session, this one only lasted two rounds. Both men now had a more positive agenda for the future and agreed to meet the next day.

Apart from the time in which he'd fulfilled his dream of working as a Spanish farmer, Peter's life had been a nightmare. The only thing the con man really knew was picking pockets, so the question now was how could he turn his wayward experience around and have a positive effect on others?

Where he once stole from unsuspecting victims, he was now going to dedicate his life to convincing the youth of the city that crime doesn't pay. Although he'd made a reasonable income during his incredible journey, Peter knew there was a better way to survive in life than by being a pickpocket.

Wasting no time, he quickly made his way across the city to set up an appointment at a youth convention—he was determined that he and Sean would do their utmost to discourage kids not to get involved in a life of crime.

Alert to the touch, he felt a delicate hand in his back pocket. Grabbing the boy's wrist, he recalled a similar situation from his long-ago past and repeated the same words: "What's your name, son?"

THE END

CONNECT WITH JOHN TRAINOR

IF YOU ENJOYED "Meet Peter the Pickpocket," please take a moment and leave a review on Amazon—they are crucial to the success of a new book. John Trainor welcomes all comments and you can connect with him via email at authorjohntrainor@gmail.com.

And before you go, you can read the first two chapters of "Meet Mowgli Muldoon," here. Watch for John's next new release!

MEET MOWGLI MULDOON

INTRODUCTION

FROM OUR EARLIEST childhood memories, a good story started with *"Once upon a time..."* and concluded with *"...and they all lived happily ever after."*

With such parameters, it certainly didn't boost an appetite to pursue more of the printed word since it was a foregone conclusion that spending time thumbing through the pages of any book would be a redundant exercise.

Well, that was the general consensus in the less-than-affluent Appalachian environment wherein young Master Muldoon's "Once upon a time..." tale began. But as we begin to discover, when he is removed from the impoverished habitat, having no choice but to take his physical challenge with him, this young man's extraordinary talents begin to surface. As for the "...happily ever after" scenario, hopefully your eyes will be opened where his weren't.

Chapter 1

HOME SWEET HOME

"JESSE HORNBECK, I'm with child."

"Woman, you said it was a good time and when I was showin' you affection you said, 'Don't worry, it's okay, Jesse, honey. Just keep goin.' I did what you asked and you assured me nothin' would happen."

Jesse's pregnant spouse was quite agitated. "Why you always say it's my fault, Jesse? You know I git with child every time you mount me, you horny horse. Don't you remember all that troubles we goin' to last time to stop all these here babies a'comin'? What kind'a medicine doctor is that Mr. Larkin, anyway? He tells us after takin' our sixty dollars we'd have no more babies. Now my belly's goin' big again."

The horny horse was not in any fit state to respond to his wife's protest or have any further discussion regarding her pregnant condition. The lack of retort was more than likely the result of the effects of the first two mugs of his home brew. This unlicensed brand of firewater was moonshine without the shine. It would have served better had it been canned and used as paint stripper.

For the Appalachian people, the main source of entertainment apart from producing babies was fiddle playing. The melodies had a definite Scottish and Irish feel, as many descendants were natives of the two countries.

As for Jesse and his wife Ruby-Jo, the music didn't exactly offer a symphony of melodic comfort or rhythm of escape from what could only be described as an overture of poverty. Having already birthed five bright-eyed children in their makeshift mansion of corrugated rust and moss-covered tin roof, they still considered themselves privileged to dwell in the camouflaged shack in the trees they called home.

Their meager piece of real estate did not offer the possibility of expansion to accommodate another arrival and no one contacted the local party planner to make arrangements to work out the finer details to celebrate the new arrival.

In this part of the country, many basic commodities that would be taken for granted in parts of the state with a slightly higher standard of living were considered a luxury. This was a home where a carpet alone was regarded as Maggiecal, like something that floated around the universe transporting a mysterious young prince in search of his soul mate.

In the back country of southern Pennsylvania there wasn't an abundance of carpets, Maggiecal or otherwise. In fact, there wasn't an abundance of anything. The employment market was another area with a definite lack of activity. Such dire circumstances promoted self-sufficiency within the tight-knit community. This was in stark contrast to those who inhabited more affluent regions of the country. In their ignorance, those who echoed the lyrics of the "Star-Spangled Banner" with their blinkered eyes, failed to understand that their brothers and sisters fell well short of the poverty line.

However, there was one man who rejected the status quo and broke free from the shackles of impoverishment in search of a better life. This journey required an abundance of faith packaged in that all-important wrapping called fortitude.

As difficult as the challenge may have been, Big Hughie was up to the task. His first undertaking was to become better acquainted with textbooks and midnight oil.

One of his most difficult challenges was not merely the struggle of obtaining an education, but to break free of the lackadaisical and laidback existence he was accustomed to. As he entered the world of academia he soon learned there was no time to be happy-go-lucky. It was more difficult for the likes of Hughie than for his classmates since most of them had been groomed for numerous years before entering the medical school arena. Hughie had no such advantage. But his determination and perseverance eventually paid dividends, earning him fellowship into the American Medical Association.

Returning to his squalid roots, he hoped his achievements would serve as a beacon of inspiration and encouragement to others. To his credit, there were no shadows of pride cast from his success.

As youngsters, after having enrolled in the dilapidated village school, it was quickly determined that best friends Jesse Hornbeck and Big Hughie's likelihood of achieving academic success bordered on the lower region of impossible. Then a bolt of scholastic lightning struck their overcrowded, institutional pale green, ramshackle classroom in the form of a mid-term staff change. Enter Miss Mary McKenna, a young, extremely attractive teacher from a very well-to-do family. Mary believed she had a spiritual calling and this divine appointment led her on a mission to raise the underdogs of the world to a more lofty status.

Her predecessor had had similar aspirations. Although an experienced educator, her involvement lasted a mere week as the challenge was far greater than she had anticipated. Those five days proved to be the worst in her teaching career.

Unprepared for the difficulties in working with these impoverished children and their lack of scholastic ability, daily frustration and exhaustion drained her enthusiasm for the job.

But the new kid on the educational block had a more determined approach and met the challenge with gusto and excitement. Recognizing a complete lack of interest on the students' expressionless faces, she determined to break through and give them hope for better days ahead, confident she could alter the status quo. Inspiring both Hughie and Jesse gave her an immediate sense of achievement, further confirming that her vocation was not in vain.

At that time, the Appalachian school system assigned a teacher to the same group of kids from the day they entered the schoolyard until the day they graduated. Only one of her star pupils chose to take full advantage of the educational opportunity.

The possibilities of a better existence lured Big Hughie Muldoon to go in search of his dream. However, his classmate and childhood companion was lured by bait of a different type. He was hooked on Ruby-Jo Kettlecat and was constantly preoccupied with the possibility of bedding the class beauty. She was, by far, the best-looking young lady not only in the school but in the entire district. Having all her teeth – which appeared to be in perfect condition when she gave one of her signature smiles – only added to her uniqueness. Her physical attributes would certainly have given her the edge with the judges had she entered the Miss Appalachia Beauty Pageant, but it would be safe to say that she might not do as well when it came to the interview segment of the contest. It was quite obvious that her inviting curves were the pinnacle of her talents.

It didn't take the fast-talking Jesse any length of time to rid the semi-illiterate, red-haired beauty of her virginity. Although it wasn't Jesse's first rodeo, he forgot the all-important golden rule: dismount prior to the achievement of complete gratification. His disobedience of the guideline proved costly. Irresponsibility for the all-pleasurable moment was a lifetime commitment to the one he had impregnated.

In fairness to the young husband-and-father-to-be, he stood by his less-than-proper actions. A contributory factor that helped him decide to do the right thing was the counseling the village stallion received from the young woman's father. Leaning on his shotgun, the possessive parent rendered his advice freely on "the ethical actions that should be taken by a horny horse."

Had Jesse chosen to ignore the sound words of the elder statesmen, the boy ran the risk of having his head blown off.

"I'm pleased to see you decided to do the right and proper thing by my Ruby-Jo and not be runnin' off with Big Hughie getting' one of those edj–u-ca-shuns. You know, young Jesse, a boy such as you should be lookin' to get some stable employment for to feed the youngsters you and my girl is goin' to be makin.'"

The fear factor caused Jesse to agree wholeheartedly with every last syllable that passed through the stained teeth of the pregnant girl's father.

"Oh, yessir, I'll do right by Ruby-Jo. I love her very much."

After accepting his father-in-law's advice, Jesse and Ruby-Jo continued to make babies, producing five beautiful sons, each of them with their father's rugged features and chiseled chin and their mother's sparkling blue eyes.

Following that fifth pregnancy, Ruby-Jo somehow convinced herself that her child-bearing days were all but gone and never in a million years thought the unexpected would happen.

It was hoped that this pregnancy was the final chapter in the family of Jesse Hornbeck and the now-less-attractive sweetheart of his youth. The local clairvoyant, Kizzy Bluebird, whom Ruby-Jo consulted on a regular basis, delivered the glad tidings from the great unknown that the much sought-after daughter they both longed for was on its way.

The no-nonsense, straight-talking Jesse said, "If Kizzy Bluebird knew all that was goin' to be takin' place, why did she not wager a bet on the local derby and pick herself the winner?"

Then correcting himself he rephrased his statement. "It be no gamble as she already knew the outcome."

"For that, my love, I do not have any such ansa, but I sure knows we goin' to have the prettiest little baby gal."

"I sure hopin' you be right or you ask old Miss Kizzy for you money back, woman."

Everyone went about their busy routine, with the five rug-rats messing up the house and their mother doing her level best to keep one step ahead cleaning up after them. As for the king of the castle, he was using all his skill to reassemble his grandfather's pocket watch after it disintegrated when he attempted to replace the winder.

An unexpected knock at the door announced that a guest had arrived on the Hornbeck doorstep. Jesse greeted the visitor. "Well, knock the brown hat off my head! If it isn't my good pal Big Hughie Muldoon. How are you, Big Hughie? Come in, you're just in time to try my new brew. It's been fermentin' for weeks. Come on and have a sample."

The polished gent politely declined the invitation to try the new-and-improved firewater explaining that he had found the Lord and did not partake of alcohol of any nature. Seeing Ruby-Jo carrying a load on her belly, Big Hughie commented, "Another boy, is it?"

Anxious to explain the situation Jesse chirped, "Well, my friend, this will be number six and Ruby-Jo recently paid a visit to old Miss Kizzy."

"Who's Miss Kizzy?" asked Hughie with a puzzled look.

"Don't you remember Charlie Bluebird?"

"Yes, I do. Did he not die down by the canyon years ago?"

Jesse confirmed Big Hughie's statement. "That was Kizzy's man. When he passed to the great unknown she got actively involved in tellin' us folks what the future has in store."

Big Hughie tried to be as tactful as possible and asked, "Jesse, you think she knows how things are going to happen before they do?"

In a very positive tone the host defended the entrepreneurial fortuneteller and said, "Oh, yes, my friend. So far, she seems to be gittin' it right. When Jimmy the farrier got that touch of the cancer, she predicted he would be leavin' us real soon, and I tell you, Hughie, in a matter of weeks I saw them lower him into the ground in the old churchyard and there was no knockin' from inside that box. The man was as dead as dead can be."

Dr. Muldoon, anxious to change the subject, said, "Peering into the future is not only satanic, but also a complete waste of time. The Lord Himself is the only one who knows what's to come, not some lonely old lady taking advantage of people by stealing their hard-earned money."

Forcing the issue, Big Hughie continued passionately, "You'd be better served throwing your pennies into that wishing well down at the creek."

"Oh, that well's no longer. The Gorman's baby fell into it losin' his sweet little life. And by the way, where was your Lord then?"

"Was that Jeremiah Gorman's baby?" asked the shocked Muldoon.

Irritated, Jesse answered, "It sure was."

In an effort to divert the verbal traffic towards a less-congested road of discussion, Big Hughie posed a question. "Is God only responsible for the bad things in life or do you think we could give him some credit for the nice things as well?"

Hughie's agenda was not to evangelize to his childhood playmate, but to give him an awareness that there are supernatural forces of good and evil and it was his belief that only good came from God.

Realizing he may have over-stayed his welcome, Hughie decided to bid the Hornbeck household a goodnight and made arrangements to meet them before he returned to the city hospital.

Muldoon's timing could be viewed as opportunistic if one was of the opinion that he did not enjoy obstetrics. The good doctor had no sooner left Jesse's house than Ruby-Jo's water broke for the sixth time. What happened next proved Kizzy the Clairvoyant was full of hot air as the long-awaited daughter was yet another bouncing baby boy.

Chapter 2

ALL THE BETTER TO SEE YOU WITH

JESSE WAS in a quandary. Caring for five was a big enough struggle and now with another mouth to feed the task looked impossible. His options were reminiscent of his kitchen pantry — both were less than plentiful. That wasn't the only challenge facing the less-than-affluent couple, either. As sad as the circumstances were, the proverbial last straw was the infant that was expected to be a beautiful blue-eyed little girl was a burly little blind boy.

"Jesse, I don't think I can take care of the ones we already have let alone another who's not seein' as good as he should."

"Woman, the boy's blind, can you not get that into your head? He ain't never goin' to see the light of day."

"How you suppose you know that? You're not a doctor like Big Hughie Muldoon."

The possessive husband exposed remnants of jealousy, detecting the sweetheart of his youth may still have feelings for the good doctor.

"You don't need to be a doctor to know that he'll never amount to nothin' when he can't see two feet in front of him."

"You never know what God can do!"

Jesse looked at Ruby-Jo as if she had just grown a pair of horns. "First, it was old Kizzy who knew it all, now it's God. Where'll you be goin' next to find out what's happenin'?"

"Jesse, I'm just sayin' we can't think the boy is no good for nothin.' We might get to be surprised."

For the sake of peace, Jesse sarcastically replied, "Whatever, woman. If he gets to become anythin,' I'm sure God or old Kizzy will be the first to know."

It didn't take long for the new parents to realize they were in well over their heads and were never going to make it. Now that another set of crying lungs and a hungry belly had joined the ranks, it was even more apparent that the strain on the already stretched budget was causing tension in every area. Having a handicapped child who needed so much attention, not to mention another mouth to feed, brought things to a head. They finally sat down at the rickety kitchen table for a closed-door discussion. After a short chit-chat, the struggling parents reached a unanimous verdict – the boy was to be sent to the state orphanage and put up for adoption.

Surprisingly, not one tear was shed by the mother who had birthed the boy. In her mind, he was a mistake, a reject. The attachment of this cruel label confirmed the lack of insight by the uneducated individuals in the deprived neighborhood.

After completing the paperwork giving consent that the child would no longer be part of the Hornbeck heritage, his father broke down, torrents of remorseful tears wetting his hard, weather-beaten face.

For months within the walls of the Hornbeck home, there was an atmosphere of grieving. Losing a child to death was one thing, but to simply give one away so freely was something that caused Jesse many days of torment and countless sleepless nights. It is often remarked that time is a great healer and to this circumstance the adage was to prove no exception, as Jesse and Ruby-Jo soon accepted that life goes on. In fact, life was beginning to take a turn for the better, the transformation being attributed to a bittersweet turn of events. The upside was that a financial nest egg was laid at their doorstep.

The price that was paid for the inheritance was that Ruby-Jo's father came out on the losing side when confronting a black bear. The contest, which wasn't much of a contest at all, was witnessed by Ruby-Jo's Uncle Dan, or as he was better known throughout the area, Dan-the-Man.

Dan's eyewitness account read... Well, it didn't read, as he could neither read nor write, but he could sure talk – his gift of gab had earned him the reputation of being the town gossip. But to his credit, his stories were usually tenable although often seasoned with a few sprinkles of exaggeration just for the sake of making the account more palatable.

"We were walking down by the riverbank shooting the breeze when out of nowhere come this angry black bear. He must've been..." Dan, being a good storyteller, paused to build the suspense. "Let me see... Yes, he must've been about twelve feet tall. Well, perhaps a little shorter. Anyway, no matter what size he was, he was certainly a big bastard. Growling like thunder, he immediately jumped on top of Ruby-Jo's Pap and for the record, I'd like to say we never gave the beast any good reason to attack. Provocation was not an excuse the beast could be using."

The reenactment caused Dan to choke with emotion. He paused to catch his breath and continued the tale. "Where was I? YES! The beast backed off for a moment and old George loaded his gun. Then the seven-feet-plus bear or whatever the hell height he was, came right back at him twice as hard. When my old friend was about to fire the gun that had been attached to his hip for as long as anybody knew him, the trigger jammed. It was all over. That's when the bear took full advantage of my helpless friend and tossed old George around like a rag doll."

If given the opportunity, Dan would have engaged his audience for the remainder of the day. But he had presented a good enough picture to stimulate their iMaggienations – they were capable of completing the scene with any details that might have been omitted.

Although the inheritance was nowhere near six figures, there were sufficient funds to make major home improvements. The first project Jesse undertook was getting rid of the outhouse. After doing the math a hundred times over he convinced himself there was enough to ensure no one was ever going to get frostbite going for a pee in the middle of a cold Appalachian winter night.

Jesse was in a dilemma, though, as to whether or not he should suggest to Ruby-Jo that they go to the orphanage and retrieve their blind son.

"Why rock the boat when things are goin' so smoothly?" he concluded.

The surprise windfall made a huge difference in their overall lifestyle, offering peace and a newfound security. Now that they didn't have the same financial struggles as before, Jesse was sympathetic and understanding towards Ruby-Jo's pining for her late father. Yet he could not reason why she never mentioned the son they had given up for adoption who was very much alive.

It seemed as if Big Hughie had no sooner left for the city than now he had returned, this time accompanied by the woman who would soon be his bride.

His first port of call was to visit his friend Jesse in the new-and-improved Hornbeck residence with its freshly painted exterior lime-washed walls and the gleaming new aluminum roof.

Jesse was tending the garden, hoping the freshly sown vegetable seeds would sprout to supply a good harvest for the harsh winters guaranteed in that region of the country.

"Don't strain that old back of yours," cajoled Hughie from the small picket fence. He then formally introduced his fiancée. "Jesse, I'd like you to meet Anne. She's also a doctor at the hospital. We work in the same department."

Jesse did his best to clean his hands before introducing himself. "It's a real pleasure, ma'am."

"Hey, Jesse, where are Ruby-Jo and the kids?" inquired Big Hughie.

"Oh, they go to her father's grave with fresh-cut flowers every Saturday. They'll be here real soon, if you'd like to wait."

"And how's the new addition doing? It was a boy, wasn't it?"

Jesse was hesitant to reply and made great efforts to change the subject.

"Yes. You here for long, Big Hughie?"

"No. Not very. We return tomorrow morning then we're off to Africa to help heal the poor unfortunate people over there."

Under his breath, Jessie said to himself, "No need to go all that ways to Africa to see poor unfortunates. Just have yourself a walk around this neighborhood. I'm sure you'll find what you're going to see in Africa minus the elephants." Although Jesse lacked a formal education, the University of Life had taught him more street savvy than the good doctor could ever possess.

No sooner had their short conversation ended than Jesse commented, "Here comes the gang."

Ruby-Jo walked along the uneven road, pushing the dilapidated perambulator with her boys hanging on every which way. This was the same one that had transported her as a child.

"Well, hello, Ruby-Jo. You look as good as ever."

At that moment, the wife of his best friend could detect the patronization in Big Hughie's tone. Her eyes immediately fixed on the woman at his side. Before the formalities of presenting the woman that would soon become his wife, an uncomfortable silence settled over the group. The source of the awkwardness was Ruby-Jo's awareness that she was being viewed in a bedraggled state – she had not expected to see Big Hughie with such an attractive and well-dressed woman.

"Please allow me to introduce to you Anne Stanfield Jones. Let me correct that; I should say Dr. Anne Stanfield Jones."

Embarrassed, Anne spoke up, "Oh, enough of your nonsense, Hugh."

Ruby-Jo extended her hand to Anne who responded by giving the downtrodden and exhausted young mother a big hug. She whispered, "You're doing such a wonderful job with all these babies. I could never do what you've done. I admire you so much, my dear."

Where Hughie's words had sounded patronizing, Anne's sounded genuine.

"I've heard so many good things about you and your husband from Hugh. I'm absolutely delighted to meet you, Ruby-Jo."

Fighting back the tears, the embarrassed Mrs. Hornbeck said, "You're very sweet. Thank you. Would you like to come in and have some fresh iced tea? I made it this mornin' before goin' to speak with my Pap."

Hearing the sincerity in Ruby-Jo's voice, Anne also struggled to refrain from crying.

Big Hughie did a quick head count and undiplomatically inquired, "Wait a minute. I'm only counting five. Where's the new addition?"

Jesse and Ruby-Jo looked at each other to see who picked the short straw to satisfy Big Hughie's curiosity. Jesse took the bull by the horns and said, "You've always had a nosy streak, Muldoon, so let me put your mind at rest. We had a son and he was born as blind as blind can be. We had no way to feed him let alone take care of all the other needs such a little nipper would require. If you really have to know, we put him up for adoption at that orphanage those Catholic people run. You know, the ones with that thick Irish accent."

Big Hughie wished he had never asked the question. Putting his hand on Jesse's shoulder, he said in a very sympathetic tone, "I completely understand, my friend."

Continuing, the leader of the Hornbeck household said, "I sure as hell hope the Good Lord above will send a sweet mammy and pappy to take good and decent care of that little unfortunate child."

In an effort to change the subject, Ruby-Jo offered the two doctors another opportunity to taste her iced tea.

"Oh, no thank you, my dear. Hugh and I have a lot of packing to do before we leave. We'll be in Africa for the next two and a half months and I have no clue what to pack."

Never one to miss an opportunity to wise crack, Jesse interjected, "I'm sure they sell toothpaste in Africa."

Matching his wit, Anne answered, "Toothpaste won't be a problem. The challenge will be rinsing our mouths with clean water as that may prove a more difficult commodity to obtain."

CPSIA information can be obtained
at www.ICGtesting.com
Printed in the USA
BVHW031144201221
624514BV00014B/85